ARSÈNE LUPIN, GENTLEMAN BURGLAR

Baron Cahorn receives a letter from Arsène Lupin, *the* gentleman burglar: master of a thousand disguises, scourge of country-houses and fashionable drawing-rooms, and nemesis of Detective Ganimard. The missive explains that Lupin has taken a fancy to various items of the baron's art and antiquities collection — with the exception of the large Watteau and the Louis XVI chatelaine, the authenticity of which appear to be 'exceedingly doubtful' — and requests that they be packed up and dispatched to him. Otherwise, he himself will see to their removal. But Arsène Lupin is presently imprisoned behind the walls of the Santé . . .

Books by Maurice Leblanc
Published by Ulverscroft:

ARSÈNE LUPIN

SPECIAL MESSAGE TO READERS

THE ULVERSCROFT FOUNDATION
(registered UK charity number 264873)
was established in 1972 to provide funds for
research, diagnosis and treatment of eye diseases.
Examples of major projects funded by
the Ulverscroft Foundation are:-

- The Children's Eye Unit at Moorfields Eye
  Hospital, London
- The Ulverscroft Children's Eye Unit at Great
  Ormond Street Hospital for Sick Children
- Funding research into eye diseases and
  treatment at the Department of Ophthalmology,
  University of Leicester
- The Ulverscroft Vision Research Group,
  Institute of Child Health
- Twin operating theatres at the Western
  Ophthalmic Hospital, London
- The Chair of Ophthalmology at the Royal
  Australian College of Ophthalmologists

You can help further the work of the Foundation
by making a donation or leaving a legacy.
Every contribution is gratefully received. If you
would like to help support the Foundation or
require further information, please contact:

THE ULVERSCROFT FOUNDATION
The Green, Bradgate Road, Anstey
Leicester LE7 7FU, England
Tel: (0116) 236 4325

website: www.foundation.ulverscroft.com

A writer of short stories for French periodicals, Maurice Leblanc was the brother of the soprano, actor and author Georgette Leblanc. When he was commissioned in 1905 to write a crime story for *Je Sais Tout*, gentleman burglar Arsène Lupin was born — bringing Leblanc critical and commercial success. In addition to this acclaimed series, Leblanc was a prolific writer of other works — including science fiction and adventure tales — and a recipient of the *Légion d'Honneur* for his services to literature.

MAURICE LEBLANC

◆

ARSÈNE LUPIN, GENTLEMAN BURGLAR

Translated from the French by
Alexander Teixeira de Mattos

Complete and Unabridged

ULVERSCROFT
Leicester

First published in France in 1907
as *Arsène Lupin, Gentleman-Cambrioleur*

This Large Print Edition
published 2016

*A catalogue record for this book is available
from the British Library.*

ISBN 978-1-4448-3011-8

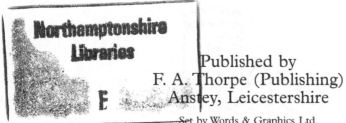

Published by
F. A. Thorpe (Publishing)
Anstey, Leicestershire
Set by Words & Graphics Ltd.
Anstey, Leicestershire
Printed and bound in Great Britain by
T. J. International Ltd., Padstow, Cornwall

This book is printed on acid-free paper

Contents

Contents

The Arrest of Arsène Lupin

The strangest of journeys! And yet it had
begun so well! I, for my part, had never made
a voyage that started under better auspices.
The *Province* is a swift and comfortable
transatlantic liner, commanded by the most
genial of men. The company gathered on
board was of a very select character.
Acquaintances were formed and amusements
organized. We had the delightful feeling of
being separated from the rest of the world,
reduced to our own devices, as though upon
an unknown island, and obliged, therefore, to
make friends with one another. And we grew
more and more intimate . . .

Have you ever reflected on the element of
originality and surprise contained in this
grouping of a number of people who, but a
day earlier, had never seen one another, and
who are now, for a few days, destined to live
together in the closest contact, between the
infinite sky and the boundless sea, defying the
fury of the ocean, the alarming onslaught of
the waves, the malice of the winds, and the
distressing calmness of the slumbering
waters?

Life itself, in fact, with its storms and its greatnesses, its monotony and its variety, becomes a sort of tragic epitome; and that, perhaps, is why we enjoy with a fevered haste and an intensified delight this short voyage of which we see the end.

But, of late years, a thing has happened that adds curiously to the excitement of the passage. The little floating island is no longer entirely separated from the world from which we believed ourselves cut adrift. One link remains, and is at intervals tied and at intervals untied in mid-ocean. The wireless telegraph! As who should say a summons from another world, whence we receive news in the most mysterious fashion! The imagination no longer has the resource of picturing wires along which the invisible message glides: the mystery is even more insoluble, more poetic; and we must have recourse to the winds to explain the new miracle.

And so, from the start, we felt that we were being followed, escorted, even preceded by that distant voice which, from time to time, whispered to one of us a few words from the continent which we had quitted. Two of my friends spoke to me. Ten others, twenty others sent to all of us, through space, their sad or cheery greetings. Now, on the stormy afternoon of the second day, when we were

2

five hundred miles from the French coast, the wireless telegraph sent us a message of the following tenor:

'Arsène Lupin on board your ship, first class, fair hair, wound on right forearm, travelling alone under alias R — '

At that exact moment, a violent thunder-clap burst in the dark sky. The electric waves were interrupted. The rest of the message failed to reach us. We knew only the initial of the name under which Arsène Lupin was concealing his identity.

Had the news been any other, I have no doubt but that the secret would have been scrupulously kept by the telegraph-clerks and the captain and his officers. But there are certain events that appear to overcome the strictest discretion. Before the day was past, though no one could have told how the rumour had got about, we all knew that the famous Arsène Lupin was hidden in our midst.

Arsène Lupin in our midst! The mysterious housebreaker whose exploits had been related in all the newspapers for months! The baffling individual with whom Ganimard, our greatest detective, had entered upon that duel to the death of which the details were being unfolded in so picturesque a fashion! Arsène Lupin, the fastidious gentleman who confines his operations to country-houses and fashionable drawing-rooms, and who one night, after breaking in at Baron Schormann's, had gone away empty-handed, leaving his visiting card:

Arsène Lupin
Gentleman Burglar

with these words added in pencil:

Will return when the furniture is genuine.

Arsène Lupin, the man with a thousand disguises, by turns chauffeur, opera-singer, book-maker, gilded youth, young man, old man, Marseillese bagman, Russian doctor, Spanish bull-fighter!

Picture the situation: Arsène Lupin moving about within the comparatively restricted compass of a transatlantic liner, nay — more, within the small space reserved to the first-class passengers — where one might come across him at any moment, in the saloon, the drawing-room, the smoking-room! Why, Arsène Lupin might be that gentleman over there . . . or this one close by . . . or my neighbour at table . . . or the passenger sharing my stateroom . . .

'And just think, this is going to last for five days!' cried Miss Nellie Underdown, on the following day. 'Why, it's awful! I do hope they'll, catch him!' And, turning to me, 'Do say, Monsieur d'Andrezy, you're such friends with the captain, haven't you heard anything?'

I wished that I had, if only to please Nellie Underdown. She was one of those magnificent creatures that become the cynosure of all eyes wherever they may be. Their beauty is as dazzling as their fortune. A court of fervent enthusiasts follow in their train.

She had been brought up in Paris by her French mother, and was now on her way to Chicago to join her father, Underdown, the American millionaire. A friend, Lady Gerland, was chaperoning her on the voyage.

I had paid her some slight attentions from the first. But, almost immediately, in the rapid intimacy of ocean travel, her charms had gained upon me, and my emotions now exceeded those of a mere flirtation whenever her great dark eyes met mine. She, on her side, received my devotion with a certain favour. She condescended to laugh at my jokes and to be interested in my stories. A vague sympathy seemed to respond to the assiduity which I displayed.

One rival alone, perhaps, could have given me cause for anxiety: a rather good-looking fellow, well-dressed and reserved in manner, slow silent humour seemed at times to attract her more than did my somewhat 'butterfly' Parisian ways.

He happened to form one of the group of admirers surrounding Miss Underdown at the moment when she spoke to me. We were on deck, comfortably installed in our chairs. The storm of the day before had cleared the sky. It was a delightful afternoon.

'I have heard nothing very definite,' I replied. 'But why should we not be able to conduct our own inquiry just as well as old Ganimard, Lupin's personal enemy, might do?'

'I say, you're going very fast!'

'Why? Is the problem so complicated?'

'Most complicated.'

'You only say that because you forget the clues which we possess towards its solution.'

'Which clues?'

'First, Lupin is travelling under the name of Monsieur R — .'

'That's rather vague.'

'Secondly, he's travelling alone.'

'If you consider that a sufficient detail!'

'Thirdly, he is fair.'

'Well, then?'

'Then we need only consult the list of first-class passengers and proceed by elimination.'

I had the list in my pocket. I took it out

and glanced through it:

'To begin with, I see that there are only thirteen persons whose names begin with an R.'

'Only thirteen?'

'In the first class, yes. Of these thirteen R's, as you can ascertain for yourself, nine are accompanied by their wives, children, or servants. That leaves four solitary passengers: the Marquis de Raverdan . . . '

'Secretary of legation,' interrupted Miss Underdown. 'I know him.'

'Major Rawson . . . '

'That's my uncle,' said someone.

'Signor Rivolta . . . '

'Here!' cried one of us, an Italian, whose face disappeared from view behind a huge black beard.

Miss Underdown had a fit of laughing. 'That gentleman is not exactly fair!'

'Then,' I continued, 'we are bound to conclude that the criminal is the last on the list.'

'Who is that?'

'Monsieur Rozaine. Does any one know Monsieur Rozaine?'

No one answered. But Miss Underdown, turning to the silent young man whose assiduous presence by her side vexed me, said:

'Well, Monsieur Rozaine, have you nothing to say?'

All eyes were turned upon him. He was fair-haired!

I must admit I felt a little shock pass through me. And the constrained silence that weighed down upon us showed me that the other passengers present also experienced that sort of choking feeling. The thing was absurd, however, for, after all, there was nothing in his manner to warrant our suspecting him.

'Have I nothing to say?' he replied. 'Well, you see, realizing what my name was and the colour of my hair and the fact that I am travelling by myself, I have already made a similar inquiry and arrived at the same conclusion. My opinion, therefore, is that I ought to be arrested.'

He wore a queer expression as he uttered these words. His thin, pale lips grew thinner and paler eyes were bloodshot.

There was no doubt but that he was jesting. And yet his appearance and attitude impressed us. Miss Underdown asked, innocently:

'But have you a wound?'

'That's true,' he said. 'The wound is missing.'

With a nervous movement, he pulled up his

cuff and uncovered his arm. But a sudden idea struck me. My eyes met Miss Underdown's: he had shown his left arm.

And, upon my word. I was on the point of remarking upon this, when an incident occurred to divert our attention. Lady Gerland, Miss Underdown's friend, came running up.

She was in a state of great agitation. Her fellow-passengers crowded round her; and it was only after many efforts that she succeeded in stammering out:

'My jewels! . . . My pearls! . . . They've all been stolen!'

No, they had not all been stolen, as we subsequently discovered; a much more curious thing had happened: the thief had made a selection!

From the diamond star, the pendant of uncut rubies, the broken necklaces and bracelets, he had removed not the largest but the finest, the most precious stones — those, in fact, which had the greatest value and at the same time occupied the smallest space. The settings were left lying on the table. I saw them, we all saw them, stripped of their gems like flowers from which the fair, bright-coloured petals had been torn.

And to carry out this work, he had had, in broad daylight, while Lady Gerland was taking tea, to break in the door of the state-room in a frequented passage, to discover a little jewel-case purposely hidden at the bottom of a bandbox, to open it and make his choice!

We all uttered the same cry. There was but one opinion among the passengers when the theft became known: it was Arsène Lupin. And, indeed, the theft had been committed in his own complicated, mysterious, inscrutable ... and yet logical manner, for we realized that, though it would have been difficult to conceal the cumbersome mass which the ornaments as a whole would have formed, he would have much less trouble with such small independent objects as single pearls, emeralds and sapphires.

At dinner this happened: the two seats to the right and left of Rozaine remained unoccupied. And, in the evening, we knew that he had been sent for by the captain.

His arrest, of which no one entertained a doubt, caused a genuine relief. We felt at last that we could breathe. We played charades in the salon. We danced. Miss Underdown, in particular, displayed an obstreperous gaiety which made it clear to me that, though Rozaine's attentions might have pleased her at first, she no longer gave them a thought. Her charm conquered me entirely. At midnight, under the still rays of the moon, I declared myself her devoted lover in emotional terms which she did not appear to resent.

But, the next day, to the general stupefaction, it became known that the charges brought against him were insufficient. Rozaine was free.

It seemed that he was the son of a wealthy Bordeaux merchant. He had produced paper's which were in perfect order. Moreover, his arms showed not the slightest trace of a wound.

'Papers, indeed!' exclaimed Rozaine's enemies. 'Birth-certificates! Tush! Why, Arsène Lupin can supply them by the dozen! As for the wound, it only shows that he never had a wound . . . or that he has removed its traces!'

Somebody suggested that, at the time when the theft was committed, Rozaine — this had been proved — was walking on deck. In reply to this it was urged that, with a man of Rozaine's stamp, it was not really necessary for the thief to be present at his own crime. And, lastly, apart from all other considerations, there was one point upon which the most sceptical had nothing to say: who but Rozaine was travelling alone, had fair hair, and was called by a name beginning with the letter R? Who but Rozaine answered to the description in the wireless telegram?

And when Rozaine, a few minutes before lunch, boldly made for our group, Lady Gerland and Miss Underdown rose and walked away.

It was a question of pure fright.

An hour later, a manuscript circular was passed from hand to hand among the staff of the vessel, the crew, and the passengers of all classes. M. Louis Rozaine had promised a reward of ten thousand francs to whosoever should unmask Arsène Lupin or discover the possessor of the stolen jewels.

'And if no one helps me against the ruffian,' said Rozaine to the captain, 'I'll settle his business myself.'

The contest between Rozaine and Arsène Lupin, or rather, in the phrase that soon became current, between Arsène Lupin himself and Arsène Lupin, was not lacking in interest.

It lasted two days. Rozaine was observed wandering to right and left, mixing with the crew, questioning and ferreting on every hand. His shadow was seen prowling about at night.

The captain, on his side, displayed the most active energy. The Provence was searched from stem to stern, in every nook and corner. Every stateroom was turned out, without exception, under the very proper pretext that the stolen objects must be hidden somewhere — anywhere rather than in the thief's own cabin.

'Surely they will end by finding something?' asked Miss Underdown. 'Wizard though he may be, he can't make pearls and diamonds invisible.'

'Of course they will,' I replied, 'or else they will have to search the linings of our hats and clothes and anything that we carry about with us.' And, showing her my five-by-four Kodak, with which I never wearied of photographing her in all manner of attitudes, I added, 'Why, even in a camera no larger than this there would be room to stow away all Lady Gerland's jewels. You pretend to take snapshots and the thing is done.'

'Still, I have heard say that every burglar always leaves a clue of some kind behind him.'

'There is one who never does: Arsène Lupin.'

'Why?'

'Why? Because he thinks not only of the crime which he is committing, but of all the circumstances that might tell against him.'

'You were more confident at first.'

'Ah, but I had not seen him at work then!'

'And so you think . . . '

'I think that we are wasting our time.'

As a matter of fact, the investigations produced no result whatever, or, at least, that which was produced did not correspond with the general effort: the captain lost his watch.

He was furious, redoubled his zeal, and kept an even closer eye than before on Rozaine, with whom he had several interviews. The next day, with a delightful irony, the watch was found among the second officer's collars.

All this was very wonderful, and pointed clearly to the humorous handiwork of a burglar, if you like, but an artist besides. He worked at his profession for a living, but also for his amusement. He gave the impression of a dramatist who thoroughly enjoys his own plays and who stands in the wings laughing heartily at the comic dialogue and diverting situations which he himself has invented.

He was decidedly an artist in his way; and, when I observed Rozaine, so gloomy and stubborn, and reflected on the two-faced part which this curious individual was doubtless playing, I was unable to speak of him without a certain feeling of admiration . . .

Well, on the night but one before our arrival in America, the officer of the watch heard groans on the darkest portion of the deck. He drew nearer, went up, and saw a man stretched at full length, with his head wrapped in a thick, grey muffler, and his hands tied together with a thin cord.

They unfastened his bonds, lifted him, and gave him a restorative.

The man was Rozaine.

Yes, it was Rozaine, who had been attacked in the course of one of his expeditions, knocked down, and robbed. A visiting-card pinned to his clothes bore these words:

Arsène Lupin accepts M. Rozaine's
ten thousand francs, with thanks.

As a matter of fact the stolen pocket-book contained twenty thousand-franc notes.

Of course, the unfortunate man was accused of counterfeiting this attack upon his own person. But, apart from the fact that it would have been impossible for him to bind himself in this way, it was proved that the writing on the card differed absolutely from Rozaine's handwriting, whereas it was exactly like that of Arsène Lupin, as reproduced in an old newspaper which had been found on board.

So Rozaine was not Arsène Lupin! Rozaine was Rozaine, the son of a Bordeaux merchant! And Arsène Lupin's presence had been asserted once again and by means of what a formidable act!

Sheer terror ensued. The passengers no longer dared stay alone in their cabins nor wander unaccompanied to the remoter parts of the ship. Those who felt sure of one another kept prudently together. And even here an instinctive mistrust divided those who knew one another best. The danger no longer threatened from a solitary individual kept under observation and therefore less dangerous. Arsène Lupin now seemed to be . . . to be everybody. Our over-excited imaginations ascribed to him the possession of a miraculous and boundless power. We supposed him capable of assuming the most unexpected disguises, of being by turns the most respectable Major Rawson, or the most noble Marquis de Raverdan, or even — for we no longer stopped at the accusing initial — this or that person known to all, and travelling with wife, children and servants.

The wireless telegrams brought us no news; at least, the captain did not communicate them to us. And this silence was not calculated to reassure us.

It was small wonder, therefore, that the last day appeared interminable. The passengers lived in the anxious expectation of a tragedy. This time it would not be a theft, it would not be a mere assault; it would be crime

— murder. No one was willing to admit that Arsène Lupin would rest content with those two insignificant acts of larceny. He was absolute master of the ship; he reduced the officers to impotence; he had but to wreak his will upon us. He could do as he pleased; he held our lives and property in his hands. These were delightful hours to me, I confess, for they won for me the confidence of Nellie Underdown. Naturally timid and impressed by all these events, she spontaneously sought at my side the protection which I was happy to offer her.

In my heart, I blessed Arsène Lupin. Was it not he who had brought us together? Was it not to him that I owed the right to abandon myself to my fondest dreams? Dreams of love and dreams more practical: why not confess it? The d'Andrezys are of good Poitevin stock, but the gilt of their blazon is a little worn; and it did not seem to me unworthy of a man of family to think of restoring the lost lustre of his name.

Nor, I was convinced, did these dreams offend Nellie. Her smiling eyes gave me leave to indulge them. Her soft voice bade me hope.

And we remained side by side until the last moment, with our elbows resting on the bulwark rail, while the outline of the American coast grew more and more distinct.

The search had been abandoned. All seemed expectation. From the first-class saloon to the steerage, with its swarm of emigrants, every one was waiting for the supreme moment when the insoluble riddle would be explained. Who was Arsène Lupin? Under what name, under what disguise was the famous Arsène Lupin lurking?

The supreme moment came. If I live to be a hundred, never shall I forget its smallest detail.

'How pale you look, Nellie!' I said, as she leaned, almost fainting, on my arm.

'And you, too. Oh, how you have changed!' she replied.

'Think what an exciting minute this is and how happy I am to pass it at your side. I wonder, Nellie, if your memory will sometimes linger . . . '

All breathless and fevered, she was not listening. The gang-plank was lowered. But before we were allowed to cross it, men came on board: custom-house officers, men in uniform, postmen.

Nellie murmured:

'I shouldn't be surprised even if we heard that Arsène Lupin had escaped during the crossing!'

'He may have preferred death to dishonour, and plunged into the Atlantic rather than submit to arrest!'

'Don't jest about it,' said she, in a tone of vexation.

Suddenly I gave a start and, in answer to her question, I replied:

'Do you see that little old man standing by the gangplank?'

'The one in a green frock-coat with an umbrella?'

'That's Ganimard.'

'Ganimard?'

'Yes, the famous detective who swore that he would arrest Arsène Lupin with his own hand. Ah, now I understand why we received no news from this side of the ocean. Ganimard was here, and he does not care to have any one interfering in his little affairs.'

'So Arsène Lupin is sure of being caught?'

'Who can tell? Ganimard has never seen him, I believe, except made-up and disguised. Unless he knows the name under which he is travelling . . . '

'Ah,' she said, with a woman's cruel curiosity, 'I should love to see the arrest!'

'Have patience,' I replied. 'No doubt Arsène Lupin has already observed his enemy's presence. He will prefer to leave among the last when the old man's eyes are tired.'

The passengers began to cross the

gangplank. Leaning on his umbrella with an indifferent air, Ganimard seemed to pay no attention to the throng that crowded past between the two hand-rails. I noticed the ship's officers, standing behind him, whispered in his ear from time to time.

The Marquis de Raverdan, Major Rawson, Rivolta, the Italian, went past, and others and many more. Then I saw Rozaine approaching.

Poor Rozaine! He did not seem to have recovered from his misadventures!

'It may be he, all the same,' said Nellie. 'What do you think?'

'I think it would be very interesting to have Ganimard and Rozaine in one photograph. Would you take the camera? My hands are so full.'

I gave it to her, but too late for her to use it. Rozaine crossed. The officer bent over to Ganimard's ear; Ganimard gave a shrug of the shoulders; and Rozaine passed on.

But then who, in Heaven's name, was Arsène Lupin?

'Yes,' she said, aloud, 'who is it!'

There were only a score of people left. Nellie looked at them, one after the other, with the bewildered dread that he was not one of the twenty.

I said to her:

'We cannot wait any longer.'

She moved on. I followed her. But we had not taken ten steps when Ganimard barred our passage.

'What does this mean?' I exclaimed.

'One moment, sir. What's your hurry?'

'I am escorting this young lady.'

'One moment,' he repeated, in a more mysterious voice.

He stared hard at me, and then, looking me straight in the eyes, said:

'Arsène Lupin, I believe.'

I gave a laugh.

'Bernard d'Andrezy, simply.'

'Bernard d'Andrezy died in Macedonia, three years ago.'

'If Bernard d'Andrezy were dead I could not be here. And it's not so. Here are my papers.'

'They are his papers. And I shall be pleased to tell you how you came to possess them.'

'But you are mad! Arsène Lupin took his passage under a name beginning with R.'

'Yes, another of your tricks — a false scent upon which you put the people on the other side, OH, you have no lack of brains, my lad! But, this time, your luck has turned. Come, Lupin, show that you're a good loser.'

I hesitated for a second. He struck me a smart blow on the right forearm. I gave a cry of pain. He had hit the unhealed wound mentioned in the telegram.

There was nothing in it but to submit. I turned to Miss Underdown. She was listening with a white face, staggering where she stood.

Her glance met mine, and then fell upon the Kodak which I had handed her. She made a sudden movement, and I received the impression, the certainty, that she had understood. Yes, it was there — between the narrow boards covered with black morocco, inside the little camera which I had taken the precaution to place in her hands before Ganimard arrested me — it was there that Rozaine's twenty thousand francs and Lady Gerland's pearls and diamonds lay concealed.

Now I swear that, at this solemn moment, with Ganimard and two of his minions around me, everything was indifferent to me — my arrest, the hostility of my fellow-men, everything save only this: the resolve which Nellie Underdown would take in regard to the object I had given into her charge.

Whether they had this material and decisive piece of evidence against me, what cared I? The only question that obsessed my mind was, would Nellie furnish it or not?

Would she betray me? Would she ruin me? Would she act as an irreconcilable foe, or as a woman who remembers, and whose contempt is softened by a touch of indulgence

— a shade of sympathy?

She passed before me. I bowed very low, without a word. Mingling with the other passengers, she moved towards the gang-board, carrying my Kodak in her hand.

'Of course,' I thought, 'she will not dare to, in public. She will hand it over presently — in an hour.'

But, on reaching the middle of the plank, with a pretended movement of awkwardness, she dropped the Kodak in the water, between the landing-stage and the ship's side.

Then I watched her walk away.

Her charming profile was lost in the crowd, came into view again, and disappeared. It was over — over for good and all.

For a moment I stood rooted to the deck, sad and, at the same time, pervaded with a sweet and tender emotion. Then, to Ganimard's great astonishment, I sighed:

'Pity, after all, that I'm a rogue!'

It was in these words that Arsène Lupin, one winter's evening, told me the story of his arrest. Chance and a series of incidents which I will some day describe had established between us bonds of . . . shall I say friendship? Yes, I venture to think that Arsène Lupin honours me with a certain friendship; and it is owing to this friendship that he occasionally drops in upon me unexpectedly, bringing into the silence of my study his youthful gaiety, the radiance of his eager life, his high spirits — the spirits of a man for whom fate has little but smiles and favours in store.

His likeness? How can I trace it? I have seen Arsène Lupin a score of times, and each time a different being has stood before me . . . or rather the same being under twenty distorted images reflected by as many mirrors, each image having its special eyes, its particular facial outline, its own gestures, profile and character.

'I myself,' he once said to me, 'have forgotten what I am really like. I no longer recognize myself in a glass.'

A paradoxical whim of the imagination, no doubt; and yet true enough as regards those who come into contact with him, and who are unaware of his infinite resources, his patience, his unparalleled skill in make-up, and his prodigious faculty for changing even the proportions of his features one to the other.

'Why,' he asked, 'should I have a definite fixed appearance? Why not avoid the dangers attendant upon a personality that is always the same? My actions constitute my identity sufficiently.'

And he added, with a touch of pride:

'It is all the better if people are never able

to say with certainty: 'There goes Arsène Lupin.' The great thing is that they should say without fear of being mistaken: 'That action was performed by Arsène Lupin.''

It is some of those actions of his, some of those exploits, that I will endeavour to narrate, thanks to the confidences with which he has had the kindness to favour me on certain winter evenings in the silence of my study . . .

Arsène Lupin in Prison

Every tourist by the banks of the Seine must have noticed, between the ruins of Jumieges and those of Saint-Wandrille, the curious little feudal castle of the Malaquis, proudly seated on its rock in mid-stream. A bridge connects it with the road. The base of its turrets seems to make one with the granite that supports it, a huge block detached from a mountain-top and flung where it stands by some formidable convulsion of nature. All around, the calm water of the broad river ripples among the reeds, while wagtails perch timidly on the top of the moist pebbles.

The history of the Malaquis is as rough as its name, as harsh as its outlines, and consists of endless fights, sieges, assaults, sacks and massacres. Stories are told in the Caux country, late at night, with a shiver, of the crimes committed there. Mysterious legends are conjured up. There is talk of a famous underground passage that led to the Abbey of Jumieges and to the manor-house of Agnes Sorel, the favourite of Charles VII.

This erstwhile haunt of heroes and robbers is now occupied by Baron Nathan

Cahorn, or Baron Satan as he used to be called on the Bourse, where he made his fortune a little too suddenly. The ruined owners of the Malaquis were compelled to sell the abode of their ancestors to him for a song. Here he installed his wonderful collections of pictures and furniture, of pottery and carvings. He lives here alone, with three old servants. No one ever enters the doors. No one has ever beheld, in the setting of those ancient halls, his three Rubens, his two Watteaus, his pulpit carved by Jean Goujon and all the other marvels snatched by force of money from before the eyes of the wealthiest frequenters of the public sale-rooms.

Baron Satan leads a life of fear. He is afraid not for himself, but for the treasures which he has accumulated with so tenacious a passion and with the perspicacity of a collector whom not the most cunning of dealers can boast of having ever taken in. He loves his curiosities with all the greed of a miser, with all the jealousy of a lover.

Daily, at sunset, the four iron-barred doors that command both ends of the bridge and the entrance to the principal court are locked and bolted. At the least touch, electric bells would ring through the surrounding silence. There is nothing to be feared on the side of the Seine, where the rock rises sheer from the water.

One Friday in September, the postman appeared as usual at the bridge-head. And, in accordance with his daily rule, the baron himself opened the heavy door.

He examined the man as closely as if he had not for years known that good jolly face and those crafty peasant eyes. And the man said, with a laugh:

'It's me all right, monsieur le baron. It's not another chap in my cap and blouse!'

'One never knows!' muttered Cahorn.

The postman handed him a bundle of newspapers. Then he added:

'And now, monsieur le baron, I have something special for you.'

'Something special? What do you mean?'

'A letter . . . and a registered letter at that!'

Living cut off from everybody, with no friends nor any one that took an interest in him, the baron never received letters; and this suddenly struck him as an ill-omened event which gave him good cause for nervousness. Who was the mysterious correspondent that came to worry him in his retreat?

'I shall want your signature, monsieur le baron.'

He signed the receipt, cursing as he did so. Then he took the letter, waited until the postman had disappeared round the turn of the road and, after taking a few steps to and fro, leaned against the parapet of the bridge and opened the envelope. It contained a sheet of ruled paper, headed, in writing:

Prison de la Santé, Paris.

He looked at the signature:

ARSÈNE LUPIN.

Utterly dumbfounded, he read:

MONSIEUR LE BARON, — *In the gallery that connects your two drawing-rooms there is a picture by Philippe de Champaigne, an excellent piece of work, which I admire greatly. I also like your Rubens pictures and the smaller of your two Watteaus. In the drawing-room on the right, I note the Louis XIII credence-table, the Beauvais tapes-tries, the Empire stand, signed by Jacob, and the Renascence chest. In the room on the left, the whole of the case of trinkets and miniatures.*

This time, I will be satisfied with these objects, which, I think, can be easily turned into cash. I will therefore ask you

to have them properly packed and to
send them to my name, carriage paid, to
the Gare de Batignolles, on or before
this day week, failing which I will myself
see to their removal on the night of
Wednesday the 27th instant. In the latter
case, as is only fair, I shall not be content with the above-mentioned objects.

Pray excuse the trouble which I am
giving you, and believe me to be

Yours very truly, ARSÈNE LUPIN

P.S. — Be sure not to send me the
larger of the two Watteaus. Although
you paid thirty thousand francs for it at
the sale-rooms, it is only a copy, the
original having been burnt under the
Directory, by Barras, in one of his
orgies. See Garat's unpublished Memoirs. I do not care either to have the
Louis XVI chatelaine, the authenticity
of which appears to me to be exceedingly doubtful.

This letter thoroughly upset Baron Cahorn. It
would have alarmed him considerably had it
been signed by any other hand. But signed by
Arsène Lupin! . . .

He was a regular reader of the newspapers,
knew of everything that went on in the way of

theft and crime and had heard all about the exploits of the infernal house-breaker. He was quite aware that Lupin had been arrested in America by his enemy, Ganimard; that he was safely under lock and key; and that the preliminaries of his trial were now being conducted . . . with great difficulty, no doubt! But he also knew that one could always expect anything of Arsène Lupin. Besides, this precise knowledge of the castle, of the arrangement of the pictures and furniture, was a very formidable sign. Who had informed Lupin of things which nobody had ever seen?

The baron raised his eyes and gazed at the frowning outline of the Malaquis, its abrupt pedestal, the deep water that surrounds it. He shrugged his shoulders. No, there was no possible danger. No one in the world could penetrate to the inviolable sanctuary that contained his collections.

No one in the world, perhaps; but Arsène Lupin? Did doors, draw-bridges, walls so much as exist for Arsène Lupin? Of what use were the most ingeniously contrived obstacles, the most skillful precautions, once that Arsène Lupin had decided to attain a given object? . . .

That same evening, he wrote to the public prosecutor at Rouen. He enclosed the threatening letter and demanded police protection.

The reply came without delay: the said Arsène Lupin was at that moment a prisoner at the Santé, where he was kept under strict observation and not allowed to write. The letter, therefore, could only be the work of a hoaxer. Everything went to prove this: logic, common sense and the actual facts. However, to make quite sure, the letter had been submitted to a handwriting expert, who declared that, notwithstanding certain points of resemblance, it was not in the prisoner's writing.

'Notwithstanding certain points of resemblance.' The baron saw only these five bewildering words, which he regarded as the confession of a doubt which alone should have been enough to justify the intervention of the police. His fears increased. He read the letter over and over again. 'I will myself see to their removal.' And that fixed date, the night of Wednesday the 27th of September!

Of a naturally suspicious and silent disposition, he dared not unburden himself to his servants, whose devotion he did not consider proof against all tests. And yet, for the first time for many years, he felt a need to speak, to take advice. Abandoned by the police of his country, he had no hope of protecting himself by his own resources and thought of going to Paris to beg for the assistance of some retired detective or other.

Two days elapsed. On the third day, as he sat reading his newspapers, he gave a start of delight. The Reveil de Caudebec contained the following paragraph:

'We have had the pleasure of numbering among our visitors, for nearly three weeks, Chief-Inspector Ganimard, one of the veterans of the detective service. M. Ganimard, for whom his last feat, the arrest of Arsène Lupin, has won a European reputation, is enjoying a rest from his arduous labours and spending a short holiday fishing for bleak and gudgeon in the Seine.'

Ganimard! The very man that Baron Cahorn wanted! Who could baffle Lupin's plans better than the cunning and patient Ganimard?

The baron lost no time. It is a four-mile walk from the castle to the little town of Caudebec. He did the distance with a quick and joyous step, stimulated by the hope of safety.

After many fruitless endeavours to discover the chief-inspector's address, he went to the office of the Reveil, which is on the quay. He found the writer of the paragraph, who, going to the window, said:

'Ganimard! Why, you're sure to meet him, rod in hand, on the quay. That's where I picked up with him and read his name, by accident, on his fishing-rod. Look, there he is, the little old man in the frock-coat and a straw hat, under the trees.'

'A frock-coat and a straw hat?'

'Yes. He's a queer specimen, close-tongued and a trifle testy.'

Five minutes later, the baron accosted the famous Ganimard, introduced himself and made an attempt to enter into conversation. Failing in this, he broached the question quite frankly and laid his case before him.

The other listened, without moving a muscle or taking his eyes from the water. Then he turned his head to the Baron, eyed him from head to foot with a look of profound compassion and said:

'Sir, it is not usual for criminals to warn the people whom they mean to rob. Arsène Lupin, in particular, never indulges in that sort of bounce.'

'Still . . .'

'Sir, if I had the smallest doubt, believe me, the pleasure of once more locking up that dear Lupin would outweigh every consideration. Unfortunately, the youth is already in prison.'

'Suppose he escapes?'

'People don't escape from the Santé.'

'But Lupin . . . '

'Lupin no more than another.'

'Still . . . '

'Very well, if he does escape, so much the better; I'll nab him again. Meanwhile, you can sleep soundly and stop frightening my fish.'

The conversation was ended. The baron returned home feeling more or less reassured by Ganimard's indifference. He saw to his bolts, kept a watch upon his servants and another forty-eight hours passed, during which he almost succeeded in persuading himself that, after all, his fears were groundless. There was no doubt about it: as Ganimard had said, criminals don't warn the people whom they mean to rob.

The date was drawing near. On the morning of Tuesday the twenty-sixth, nothing particular happened. But, at three o'clock in the afternoon, a boy rang and handed in this telegram:

No goods Batignolles. Get everything ready for to-morrow night. ARSÈNE.

Once again, Cahorn lost his head, so much so that he asked himself whether he would not do better to yield to Arsène Lupin's demands.

35

He hurried off to Caudebec. Ganimard was seated on a camp-stool, fishing, in the same spot as before. The baron handed him the telegram without a word.

'Well?' said the detective.

'Well what? It's fixed for tomorrow!'

'What is?'

'The burglary! The theft of my collections!'

Ganimard turned to him, and, folding his arms across his chest, cried, in a tone of impatience:

'Why, you don't really mean to say that you think I'm going to trouble myself about this stupid business?'

'What fee will you take to spend Wednesday night at the castle?'

'Not a penny. Don't bother me!'

'Name your own price. I'm a rich man, a very rich man.'

The brutality of the offer took Ganimard aback. He replied, more calmly:

'I am here on leave and I have no right to . . . '

'No one shall know. I undertake to be silent, whatever happens!'

'Oh, nothing will happen!'

'Well, look here; is three thousand francs enough?'

The inspector took a pinch of snuff, reflected and said:

'Very well. But it's only fair to tell you that you are throwing your money away.'

'I don't mind.'

'In that case . . . And besides, after all, one can never tell, with that devil of a Lupin! He must have a whole gang at his orders . . . Are you sure of your servants?'

'Well, I . . . '

'Then we must not rely upon them. I'll wire to two of my own men; that will make us feel safer . . . And, now, leave me; we must not be seen together. Tomorrow evening, at nine o'clock.'

On the morning of the next day, the date fixed by Arsène Lupin, Baron Cahorn took down his trophy of arms, polished up his pistols and made a thorough inspection of the Malaquis, without discovering anything suspicious.

At half-past eight in the evening, he dismissed his servants for the night. They slept in a wing facing the road, but set a little way back and right at the end of the castle. As soon as he was alone, he softly opened the four doors. In a little while, he heard footsteps approaching.

Ganimard introduced his assistants, two powerfully-built fellows, with bull necks and huge, strong hands, and asked for certain explanations. After ascertaining the disposition of the place, he carefully closed and barricaded every issue by which the threatened rooms could be entered. He examined the walls, lifted up the tapestries and finally installed his detectives in the central gallery. 'No nonsense, do you understand? You're not here to sleep. At the least sound, open the windows on the court and call me. Keep a look-out also on the water side. Thirty feet of steep cliff doesn't frighten scoundrels of that stamp.'

He locked them in, took away the keys and said to the baron:

'And now to our post.'

He had selected, as the best place in which to spend the night, a small room contrived in the thickness of the outer walls, between the two main doors. It had at one time been the watchman's lodge. A spy-hole opened upon the bridge, another upon the court. In one corner was what looked like the mouth of a well.

'You told me, did you not, monsieur le baron, that this well is the only entrance to the underground passage and that it has been stopped up since the memory of man?'

'Yes.'

'Therefore, unless there should happen to be another outlet, unknown to any but Arsène Lupin, which seems pretty unlikely, we can be easy in our minds.'

He placed three chairs in a row, settled himself comfortably at full length, lit his pipe and sighed:

'Upon my word, monsieur le baron, I must be very eager to build an additional storey to the little house in which I mean to end my days, to accept so elementary a job as this. I shall tell the story to our friend Lupin; he'll split his sides with laughter.'

The baron did not laugh. With ears pricked up, he questioned the silence with ever-growing restlessness. From time to time, he leaned over the well and plunged an anxious eye into the yawning cavity.

The clock struck eleven; midnight; one o'clock.

Suddenly, he seized the arm of Ganimard, who woke with a start:

'Do you hear that?'

'Yes.'

'What is it?'

'It's myself, snoring!'

'No, no, listen . . . '

'Oh yes, it's a motor-horn.'

'Well?'

'Well, it's as unlikely that Lupin should come by motor-car as that he should use a battering-ram to demolish your castle. So I should go to sleep, if I were you, monsieur le baron . . . as I shall have the honour of doing

39

once more. Good-night!'

This was the only alarm. Ganimard resumed his interrupted slumbers; and the baron heard nothing save his loud and regular snoring.

At break of day, they left their cell. A great calm peace, the peace of the morning by the cool waterside, reigned over the castle. Cahorn, beaming with joy, and Ganimard, placid as ever, climbed the staircase. Not a sound. Nothing suspicious.

'What did I tell you, monsieur le baron? I really ought not to have accepted . . . I feel ashamed of myself . . . '

He took the keys and entered the gallery.

On two chairs, with bent bodies and hanging arms, sat the two detectives, fast asleep.

'What, in the name of all the . . . ' growled the inspector.

At the same moment, the baron uttered a cry:

'The pictures! . . . The credence-table!'

He stammered and spluttered, with his hand out-stretched towards the dismantled walls, with their bare nails and slack cords. The Watteau and the two Rubens had disappeared! The tapestries had been removed, the glass cases emptied of their trinkets!

'And my Louis XVI sconces! . . . And the Regency chandelier! . . . And my twelfth-century Virgin! . . . '

He ran from place to place, maddened, in despair. Distraught with rage and grief, he quoted the purchase-prices, added up his losses, piled up figures, all promiscuously, in indistinct words and incomplete phrases. He stamped his feet, flung himself about and, in short, behaved like a ruined man who had nothing before him but suicide.

If anything could have consoled him, it would have been the sight of Ganimard's stupefaction. Contrary to the baron, the inspector did not move. He seemed petrified, and with a dazed eye, examined things. The windows? They were fastened. The locks of the doors? Untouched. There was not a crack in the ceiling, not a hole in the floor. Everything was in perfect order. The whole thing must have been carried out methodically, after an inexorable and logical plan.

'Arsène Lupin . . . Arsène Lupin,' he muttered, giving way.

Suddenly, he leapt upon the two detectives, as though at last overcome with rage, and shook them and swore at them furiously. They did not wake up!

'The deuce!' he said. 'Can they have been . . . ?'

He bent over them and scrutinized them closely, one after the other: they were both asleep, but their sleep was not natural. He said to the baron:

'They have been drugged.'

'But by whom?'

'By him, of course . . . or by his gang, acting under his instructions. It's a trick in his own manner. I recognize his touch.'

'In that case, I am undone: the thing is hopeless.'

'Hopeless.'

'But this is abominable; it's monstrous.'

'Lodge a complaint.'

'What's the good?'

'Well, you may as well try . . . the law has its resources . . . '

'The law! But you can see for yourself . . . Why, at this very moment, when you might be looking for a clue, discovering something, you're not even stirring!'

'Discover something, with Arsène Lupin! But, my dear sir, Arsène Lupin never leaves anything behind him! There's no chance with Arsène Lupin! I am beginning to wonder whether he got himself arrested by me of his own free will, in America!'

'Then I must give up the hope of recovering my pictures or anything! But he has stolen the pearls of my collection. I would give a fortune to get them back. If there's nothing to be done against him, let him name his price.'

Ganimard looked at him steadily:

'That's a sound notion. Do you stick to it?'

'Yes, yes, yes! But why do you ask?'

'I have an idea.'

'What idea?'

'We'll talk of it if nothing comes of the inquiry . . . Only, not a word about me, to a soul, if you wish me to succeed.'

And he added, between his teeth:

'Besides, I have nothing to be proud of.'

The two men gradually recovered consciousness, with the stupefied look of men awakening from an hypnotic sleep. They opened astounded eyes, tried to make out what had happened. Ganimard questioned them. They remembered nothing.

'Still you must have seen somebody?'

'No, nobody.'

'Try and think?'

'No, nobody.'

'Did you have a drink?'

They reflected and one of them replied:

'Yes, I had some water.'

'Out of that bottle there?'

'Yes.'

'I had some too,' said the other.

Ganimard smelt the water, tasted it. It had

43

no particular scent or favour.

'Come', he said, 'we are wasting our time. Problems set by Arsène Lupin can't be solved in five minutes. But, by Jingo, I swear I'll catch him! He's won the second bout. The rubber game to me!'

That day, a charge of aggravated larceny was brought by Baron Cahorn against Arsène Lupin, a prisoner awaiting trial at the Santé.

The baron often regretted having laid his information when he saw the Malaquis made over to the gendarmes, the public prosecutor, the examining magistrate, the newspaper-reporters and all the inquisitive who worm themselves in wherever they have no business to be.

Already the case was filling the public mind. It had taken place under such peculiar conditions and the name of Arsène Lupin excited men's imaginations to such a pitch that the most fantastic stories crowded the columns of the press and found acceptance with the public.

But the original letter of Arsène Lupin, which was published in the Echo de France — and no one ever knew who had supplied the text — the letter in which Baron Cahorn was insolently warned of what threatened him, caused the greatest excitement. Fabulous explanations were offered forthwith. The old legends were revived. The newspapers reminded their readers of the existence of the famous subterranean passages. And the public prosecutor, influenced by these statements, pursued his search in that direction.

The castle was ransacked from top to bottom. Every stone was examined; the wainscotings and chimneys, the frames of the mirrors and the rafters of the ceilings were carefully inspected. By the light of torches, the searchers investigated the immense cellars in which the lords of the Malaquis had been used to pile up their provisions and munitions of war. They sounded the very bowels of the rock. All to no purpose. They discovered not the slightest trace of a tunnel. No secret passage existed.

Very well, was the answer on every side; but pictures and furniture don't vanish like ghosts. They go out through doors and windows; and the people that take them also go in and out through doors and windows. Who are these people? How did they get in? And how did they get out?

The public prosecutor of Rouen, persuaded of his own incompetence, asked for the assistance of the Paris police. M. Dudouis, the chief of the detective-service, sent the most efficient bloodhounds in his employ. He himself paid a forty-eight hours' visit to the Malaquis, but met with no greater success.

It was after his return that he sent for Chief-Inspector Ganimard, whose services he had so often had occasion to value.

Ganimard listened in silence to the instructions of his superior and then, tossing his head, said:

'I think we shall be on a false scent so long as we continue to search the castle. The solution lies elsewhere.'

'With Arsène Lupin? If you think that, then you believe that he took part in the burglary.'

'I do think so. I go further, I consider it certain.'

'Come, Ganimard, this is absurd. Arsène Lupin is in prison.'

'Arsène Lupin is in prison, I agree. He is being watched, I grant you. But, if he had his legs in irons, his hands bound and his mouth gagged, I should still be of the same opinion.'

'But why this persistency?'

'Because no one else is capable of contriving a plan on so large a scale and of contriving it in such a way that it succeeds . . . as this has succeeded.'

'Words, Ganimard!'

'They are true words, for all that. Only, it's no use looking for underground passages, for stones that turn on a pivot and stuff and nonsense of that kind. Our friend does not employ such antiquated measures. He is a man of to-day, or rather of tomorrow'

'And what do you conclude?'

'I conclude by asking you straight to let me spend an hour with Lupin.'

'In his cell?'

'Yes. We were on excellent terms during the crossing from America and I venture to think that he is not without friendly feeling for the man who arrested him. If he can tell me what I want to know, without compromising himself, he will be quite willing to spare me an unnecessary journey.'

It was just after mid-day when Ganimard was shown into Arsène Lupin's cell. Lupin, who was lying on his bed, raised his head and uttered an exclamation of delight:

'Well, this is a surprise! Dear old Ganimard here!'

'Himself.'

'I have hoped for many things in this retreat of my own choosing, but for none more eagerly than the pleasure of welcoming you here.'

'You are too good.'

'Not at all, not at all. I have the liveliest regard for you.'

'I am proud to hear it.'

'I have said it a thousand times: Ganimard

is our greatest detective. He's almost — see how frank I am — almost as clever as Sherlock Holmes. But, really, I'm awfully sorry to have nothing better than this stool to offer you. And not a drink of any kind! Not so much as a glass of beer! Do forgive me: I am only just passing through town, you see!'

Ganimard smiled and sat down on the stool; and the prisoner, glad of the opportunity of speaking, continued:

'By Jove, what a treat to see a decent man's face! I am sick of the looks of all these spies who go through my cell and my pockets ten times a day to make sure that I am not planning an escape. Fichtre! how fond the government must be of me!'

'They show their judgment.'

'No, no! I should be so happy if they would let me lead my own quiet life.'

'On other people's money.'

'Just so. It would be so simple. But I'm letting my tongue run on, I'm talking nonsense and I daresay you're in a hurry. Come, Ganimard, tell me to what I owe the honour of this visit.'

'The Cahorn case,' said Ganimard, abruptly.

'Stop! Wait a bit . . . You see, I have so many on hand! First, let me search my brain for the Cahorn pigeonhole . . . Ah, I have it!

Cahorn case, Chateau du Malaquis, Seine-Inferieure . . . Two Rubens, a Watteau and a few minor trifles.'

'Trifles!'

'Oh, yes, all this is of small importance. I have bigger things on hand. However, you're interested in the case and that's enough for me . . . Go ahead, Ganimard.'

'I need not tell you, need I, how far we have got with the investigation?'

'No, not at all. I have seen the morning papers. And I will even take the liberty of saying that you are not making much progress.'

'That's just why I have come to throw myself upon your kindness.'

'I am entirely at your service.'

'First of all, the thing was done by you, was it not?'

'From start to finish.'

'The registered letter? The telegram?'

'Were sent by yours truly. In fact, I ought to have the receipts somewhere.'

Arsène opened the drawer of a little deal table which, with the bed and the stool, composed all the furniture of his cell, took out two scraps of paper and handed them to Ganimard.

'Hullo!' cried the latter. 'Why, I thought you were being kept under constant observation and searched on the slightest pretext.

And it appears that you read the papers and collect post-office receipts . . . '

'Bah! Those men are such fools. They rip up the lining of my waistcoat, explore the soles of my boots, listen at the walls of my cell; but not one of them would believe that Arsène Lupin could be such a fool as to choose so obvious a hiding-place. That's just what I reckoned on.'

Ganimard exclaimed, in amusement:

'What a funny chap you are! You're beyond me. Come, tell me the story.'

'Oh, I say! Not so fast! Initiate you into all my secrets . . . reveal my little tricks to you? That's a serious matter.'

'Was I wrong in thinking that I could rely on you to oblige me?'

'No, Ganimard, and, as you insist upon it . . . '

Arsène Lupin took two or three strides across his cell. Then, stopping:

'What do you think of my letter to the baron?' he asked.

'I think you wanted to have some fun, to tickle the gallery a bit.'

'Ah, there you go! Tickle the gallery, indeed! Upon my word, Ganimard, I gave you credit for more sense! Do you really imagine that I, Arsène Lupin, waste my time with such childish pranks as that? Is it likely that I should have written the letter, if I could have rifled the baron without it? Do try and understand that the letter was the indispensable starting-point, the main-spring that set the whole machine in motion. Look here, let us proceed in order and, if you like, prepare the Malaquis burglary together.'

'Very well.'

'Now follow me. I have to do with an impregnable and closely-guarded castle . . . Am I to throw up the game and forego the treasures which I covet, because the castle that contains them happens to be inaccessible?'

'Clearly not.'

'Am I to try to carry it by assault as in the old days, at the head of a band of adventurers?'

'That would be childish.'

'Am I to enter it by stealth?'

'Impossible.'

'There remains only one way, which is to get myself invited by the owner of the foresaid castle.'

'It's an original idea.'

'And so easy! Suppose that, one day, the said owner receives a letter warning him of a plot hatched against him by one Arsène Lupin, a notorious housebreaker. What is he sure to do?'

'Send the letter to the public prosecutor.'

'Who will laugh at him, because the said Lupin is actually under lock and key. The natural consequence is the utter bewilderment of the worthy man, who is ready and anxious to ask for the assistance of the first-comer. Am I right?'

'Quite so.'

'And, if he happens to read in the local rag that a famous detective is staying in the neighbourhood . . . ?'

'He will go and apply to that detective.'

'Exactly. But, on the other hand, let us assume that, foreseeing this inevitable step, Arsène Lupin has asked one of his ablest friends to take up his quarters at Caudebec, to pick up acquaintance with a contributor to the Reveil, a paper, mark you, to which the baron subscribes, and to drop a hint that he is so-and-so, the famous detective. What will happen next?'

'The contributor will send a paragraph to the Reveil stating that the detective is staying at Caudebec.'

'Exactly; and one of two things follows; either the fish — I mean Cahorn — does not rise to the bait, in which case nothing happens. Or else — and this is the more likely presumption — he nibbles, in which case you have our dear Cahorn imploring the assistance of one of my own friends against me!'

'This is becoming more and more original.'

'Of course, the sham detective begins by refusing. Thereupon, a telegram from Arsène Lupin. Dismay of the baron, who renews his entreaties with my friend and offers him so much to watch over his safety. The friend aforesaid accepts and brings with him two chaps of our gang, who, during the night, while Cahorn is kept in sight by his protector, remove a certain number of things through the window and lower them with ropes into a barge freighted for the purpose. It's as simple as . . . Lupin.'

'And it's just wonderful,' cried Ganimard, 'and I have no words in which to praise the boldness of the idea and the ingenuity of the details. But I can hardly imagine a detective so illustrious that his name should have attracted and impressed the baron to that extent.'

'There is one and one only.'

'Who?'

'The most illustrious of them all, the arch-enemy of Arsène Lupin, in short, Inspector Ganimard.'

'What, myself?'

'Yourself, Ganimard. And that's the

delightful part of it: if you go down and persuade the baron to talk, he will end by discovering that it is your duty to arrest yourself, just as you arrested me in America. A humorous revenge, what? I shall have Ganimard arrested by Ganimard!'

Arsène Lupin laughed loud and long, while the inspector bit his lips with vexation. The joke did not appear to him worthy of so much merriment.

The entrance of a warder gave him time to recover. The man brought the meal which Arsène Lupin, by special favour, was allowed to have sent in from the neighbouring restaurant. After placing the tray on the table, he went away. Arsène sat down, broke his bread, ate a mouthful or two and continued:

'But be easy, my dear Ganimard, you won't have to go. I have something to tell you that will strike you dumb. The Cahorn case is about to be withdrawn.'

'What!'

'About to be withdrawn, I said.'

'Nonsense! I have just left the chief.'

'And then? Does Monsieur Dudouis know more than I do about my concerns? You must learn that Ganimard — excuse me — that the sham Ganimard remained on very good terms with Baron Cahorn. The baron — and this is his main reason for keeping the thing quiet — charged him with the very delicate mission of negotiating a deal with me; and the chances are that, by this time, on payment of a certain sum, the baron is once more in possession of his pet knick-knacks. In return for which he will withdraw the charge. Wherefore there is no question of theft. Wherefore the public prosecutor will have to abandon . . .'

Ganimard gazed at the prisoner with an air of stupefaction:

'But how do you know all this?'

'I have just received the telegram I was expecting.'

'You have just received a telegram?'

'This very moment, my friend. I was too polite to read it in your presence. But, if you will allow me . . .'

'You're poking fun at me, Lupin.'

'Have the kindness, my friend, to cut off the top of that egg, gently. You will see for yourself that I am not poking fun at you.'

Ganimard obeyed mechanically and broke the egg with the blade of a knife. A cry of surprise escaped him. The shell was empty but for a sheet of blue paper. At Arsène's request, he unfolded it. It was a telegram, or rather a portion of a telegram from which the postal indications had been removed. He read:

Arrangement settled. Hundred thousand
spondulics delivered. All well.

'Hundred thousand spondulics?' he uttered.

'Yes, a hundred thousand francs. It's not much, but these are hard times . . . And my general expenses are so heavy! If you knew the amount of my budget . . . it's like the budget of a big town!'

Ganimard rose to go. His ill-humour had left him. He thought for a few moments and cast a mental glance over the whole business, trying to discover a weak point. Then, in a voice that frankly revealed his admiration as an expert, he said:

'It's a good thing that there are not dozens like you, or there would be nothing for us but to shut up shop.'

Arsène Lupin assumed a modest simper and replied:

'Oh, I had to do something to amuse myself, to occupy my spare time . . . especially as the scoop could only succeed while I was in prison.'

'What do you mean?' exclaimed Ganimard. 'Your trial, your defence, your examination: isn't that enough for you to amuse yourself with?'

'No, because I have decided not to attend my trial.'

'Oh, I say!'

Arsène Lupin repeated deliberately:

'I shall not attend my trial.'

'Really!'

'Why, my dear fellow, you surely don't think I mean to rot in gaol? The mere suggestion is an insult. Let me tell you that Arsène Lupin remains in prison as long as he thinks fit and not a moment longer.'

'It might have been more prudent to begin by not entering it,' said the inspector, ironically.

'Ah, so you're chaffing me, sirrah? Do you remember that you had the honour to effect my arrest? Well, learn from me, my respectable friend, that no one, neither you nor another, could have laid a hand upon me, if a much more important interest had not occupied my attention at that critical moment.'

'You surprise me.'

'A woman had cast her eyes upon me, Ganimard, and I loved her. Do you realize all that the fact implies when a woman whom one loves casts her eyes upon one? I cared about little else, I assure you. And that is why I'm here.'

'You've been here a long time, allow me to observe.'

'I was anxious to forget. Don't laugh, it was

a charming adventure and I still have a tender recollection of it . . . And then I have had a slight nervous break-down. We lead such a feverish existence nowadays! It's a good thing to take a rest-cure from time to time. And there's no place for it like this. They carry out the cure in all its strictness at the Santé.'

'Arsène Lupin,' said Ganimard, 'you're pulling my leg.'

'Ganimard,' replied Lupin, 'this is Friday. On Wednesday next, I'll come and smoke a cigar with you, in the Rue Pergolese, at four o'clock in the afternoon.'

'Arsène Lupin, I shall expect you.'

They shook hands like two friends who have a proper sense of each other's value and the old detective turned towards the door.

'Ganimard!'

Ganimard looked round:

'What is it?'

'Ganimard, you've forgotten your watch.'

'My watch?'

'Yes, I've just found it in my pocket.'

He returned it, with apologies:

'Forgive me . . . it's a bad habit . . . They've taken mine, but that's no reason why I should rob you of yours. Especially as I have a chronometer here which keeps perfect time and satisfies all my requirements.'

He took out of the drawer a large, thick,

comfortable-looking gold watch, hanging to a heavy chain.

'And out of whose pocket does this come?' asked Ganimard.

Arsène Lupin carelessly inspected the initials:

'J.B . . . What on earth does that stand for? . . . Oh, yes, I remember: Jules Bouvier, my examining magistrate, a charming fellow . . . '

The Escape of Arsène Lupin

Arsène Lupin finished his mid-day meal, took a good cigar from his pocket, and complacently studied the gold-lettered inscription on its band. At that moment the door of his cell opened. He had just a second in which to throw the cigar into the drawer of the table and to move away. The warden came in to tell him that it was time to take his exercise.

'I was waiting for you, old chap!' cried Lupin, with his unfailing good-humour.

They went out together. Hardly had they turned the corner of the passage when two men entered the cell and began to make a minute examination. One of these was Inspector Dieuzy, the other Inspector Folenfant.

They wanted to have the matter settled once and for all. There was no doubt about it: Arsène Lupin was keeping up a correspondence with the outside world and communicating with his confidants. Only the day before the Grand Journal had published the following lines, addressed to its legal contributor:

SIR, — In an article published a few days ago you ventured to express yourself concerning me in utterly unwarrantable terms. I shall come and call you to account a day or two before my trial commences. Yours faithfully,
ARSÈNE LUPIN.

The handwriting was Arsène Lupin's. Therefore, he was sending letters. Therefore, he was receiving letters. Therefore, it was certain that he was preparing the escape which he had so arrogantly announced.

The position was becoming intolerable. By arrangement with the examining magistrate, M. Dudouis himself, the head of the detective service, went to the Santé to explain to the prison governor the measures which it was thought advisable to take, and on his arrival he sent two of his men to the prisoner's cell.

The men raised every one of the flag-stones, took the bed to pieces, did all that is usually done in such cases, and ended by discovering nothing. They were about to abandon their search when the warden came running in, and said:

'The drawer . . . look in the drawer of the table! I thought I saw him shut it when I came in just now.'

They looked, and Dieuzy exclaimed:

'Gad, we've caught our customer this time!'

Folenfant stopped him.

'Don't do anything, my lad; let the chief take the inventory.'

'Still, this Havana . . . '

'Leave it alone, and let us tell the chief.'

Two minutes later M. Dudouis was exploring the contents of the drawer. He found, first, a collection of press-cuttings concerning Arsène Lupin; next, a tobacco-pouch, a pipe, and some foreign post-paper; and, lastly, two books.

He looked at the titles: Carlyle's *Heroes and Hero-Worship*, in English, and a charming Elsevier, in the contemporary binding: a German translation of the *Manual of Epictetus*, published at Leyden in 1634. He glanced through them, and observed that every page was scored, underlined, and annotated. Were these conventional signs, or were they marks denoting the reader's devotion to a particular book?

'We'll go into this in detail,' said M. Dudouis.

He investigated the tobacco-pouch, the pipe. Then, taking up the magnificent cigar in its gold band:

'By Jove!' he cried, 'our friend does himself well! A Henry Clay!'

With the mechanical movement of a smoker he put it to his ear and crackled it. An exclamation escaped him. The cigar had given way under the pressure of his fingers! He examined it more attentively, and soon perceived something that showed white between the leaves of the tobacco. And carefully, with the aid of a pin, he drew out a scroll of very thin paper, no thicker than a tooth-pick. It was a note. He unrolled it, and read the following words, in a small, female hand:

Maria has taken the other's place. Eight out of ten are prepared. On pressing outside foot, metal panel moves upward. H.P. will wait from 12 to 16 daily. But where? Reply at once. Have no fear: your friend is looking after you.

M. Dudouis reflected for a moment and said:

'That's clear enough . . . Maria, the prison-van . . . the eight compartments . . . Twelve to sixteen; that is, from twelve to four o'clock . . . '

'But who is H.P.? Who is to wait for him?'

'H.P. stands for horse-power, of course — a motor-car.'

He rose and asked:

'Had the prisoner finished his lunch?'

'Yes.'

'And, as he has not yet read this message, as the condition of the cigar shows, the chances are that he had only just received it.'

'By what means?'

'How can I tell? In his food; inside a roll or a potato.'

'That's impossible. He was only permitted to have his meals from the outside so that we might trap him and we have found nothing.'

'We will look for Lupin's reply this evening. Meantime keep him out of his cell. I will take this to Monsieur Bouvier, the examining magistrate. If he agrees, we will have the letter photographed at once, and in an hour's time you can put these other things back in the drawer, together with an exactly similar cigar containing the original message. The prisoner must not be allowed to suspect anything.'

It was not without a certain curiosity that M. Dudouis, accompanied by Inspector Dieuzy, returned to the office of the Santé in the evening. In a corner, on the stove, were three plates.

'Has he had his dinner?'

'Yes,' replied the governor.

'Dieuzy, cut those pieces of macaroni into very thin shreds and open that bit of bread . . . Is there nothing there?'

'No, sir.'

M. Dudouis examined the plates, the fork, the spoon, and, lastly, the knife — a regulation knife with a rounded blade. He twisted the handle to the left and then to the right. When turned to the right the handle gave way and became unscrewed. The knife was hollow, and served as a sheath for a slip of paper.

'Pooh!' he said, 'that's not very artful for a man like Arsène. But let us waste no time. Do you go to the restaurant, Dieuzy, and make your inquiries.'

Then he read:

I leave it to you. Let H.P. follow every day at a distance. I shall go in front. I shall see you soon, my dear and adorable friend.

'At last!' cried M. Dudouis, rubbing his hands. 'Things are going better, I think. With a little assistance from our side the escape will succeed . . . Just enough to enable us to bag the accomplices.'

'And suppose Arsène Lupin slips through your fingers?' said the governor.

'We shall employ as many men as are necessary. If, however, he shows himself too clever . . . well, then, so much the worse for him! As for the rest of the gang, since the leader refuses to talk the others must be made to.'

The fact was that Arsène Lupin did not talk much. For some months M. Jules Bouvier, the examining magistrate, had been exerting himself to no purpose. The interrogatories were reduced to uninteresting colloquies between the magistrate and Maitre Danval, one of the leaders of the bar, who, for that matter, knew as much and as little about the defendant as the man in the street.

From time to time, out of politeness, Arsène Lupin would let fall a remark:

'Quite so, sir; we are agreed. The robbery at the Credit Lyonnais, the robbery in the Rue de Babylone, the uttering of the forged notes, the affair of the insurance policies, the burglaries at the Chateaux d'Armesnil, de Gouret, d'Imblevain, des Groseillers, du Malaquis: that's all my work.'

'Then perhaps you will explain . . . '

'There's no need of it. I confess to everything in the lump — everything, and ten times as much.'

Tired out, the magistrate had suspended these wearisome interrogatories. He resumed them, after being shown the two intercepted missives. And regularly at twelve o'clock every day Arsène Lupin was taken from the Santé to the police-station in a van, with a number of other prisoners. They left again at three or four in the day.

One afternoon the return journey took place under exceptional conditions. As the other criminals from the Santé had not yet been examined, it was decided to take Arsène Lupin back first. He therefore stepped into the van alone.

These prison-vans, vulgarly known as paniers a salade, or salad-baskets, in France, and as 'Black Marias' in England, are divided lengthwise by a central passage, giving admittance to ten compartments or boxes, five on each side. Each of these boxes is so arranged that its occupant has to adopt a sitting posture, and the five prisoners are consequently seated one beside the other, and are separated by parallel partitions. A municipal guard sits at the end and watches the central passage.

Arsène was placed in the third box on the right, and the heavy vehicle started. He perceived that they had left the Quai de l'Horloge, and were passing before the Palais de Justice. When they reached the middle of the Pont Saint-Michel he pressed his outer foot — that is to say, his right foot, as he had always done — against the sheet-iron panel that closed his cell. Suddenly something was thrown out of gear, and the panel opened outward imperceptibly. He saw that he was just between the two wheels.

He waited, with a watchful eye. The van went along the Boulevard Saint-Michel at a foot's pace. At the Carrefour Saint-Germain it pulled up. A dray-horse had fallen. The traffic was stopped, and soon there was a block of cabs and omnibuses.

Arsène Lupin put out his head. Another prison-van was standing beside the one in which he was sitting. He raised the panel farther, put his foot on one of the spokes of the hind wheel, and jumped to the ground.

A cab-driver saw him, choked with laughing, and then tried to call out. But his voice was lost in the din of the traffic, which had started afresh. Besides, Arsène Lupin was already some distance away.

He had taken a few steps at a run; but, crossing to the left-hand pavement, he turned back, cast a glance around him, and seemed to be taking his breath, like a man who is not quite sure which direction he means to follow. Then, making up his mind, he thrust his hands into his pockets, and, with the careless air of a person taking a stroll, continued to walk along the boulevard.

The weather was mild: it was a bright, warm autumn day. The cafes were full of people. He sat down outside one of them.

He called for a bock and a packet of cigarettes. He emptied his glass with little sips, calmly smoked a cigarette and lit a second. Lastly, he stood up and asked the waiter to fetch the manager.

The manager came, and Arsène said, in a voice loud enough to be heard by all around:

'I am very sorry, but I have come out without my purse. Possibly you know my name and will not mind trusting me for a day or two: I am Arsène Lupin.'

The manager looked at him, thinking he was joking. But Arsène repeated:

'Lupin, a prisoner at the Santé, recently escaped. I venture to hope that my name inspires you with every confidence.'

And he walked away amid the general laughter before the other dreamed of raising a protest.

He slanted across the Rue Soufflot, and turned down the Rue Saint-Jacques. He proceeded along this street quietly, looking at the shop-windows, and smoking one cigarette after the other. On reaching the Boulevard de Port-Royal he took his bearings, asked the way, and walked straight towards the Rue de la Santé. Soon the frowning walls of the prison came into view. He skirted them, and, going up to the municipal guard who was standing sentry at the gate, raised his hat, and said:

'Is this the Santé Prison?'

'Yes.'

'I want to go back to my cell, please. The van dropped me on the way, and I should not like to abuse . . . '

The guard grunted.

'Look here, my man, you just go your road, and look sharp about it!'

'I beg your pardon, but my road lies through this gate. And, if you keep Arsène Lupin out, it may cost you dear, my friend.'

'Arsène Lupin! What's all this?'

'I am sorry I haven't a card on me,' said Arsène, pretending to feel in his pockets.

The guard, utterly nonplussed, eyed him from head to foot. Then, without a word and as though in spite of himself, he rang a bell. The iron door opened.

A few minutes later the governor hurried into the office, gesticulating and pretending to be in a violent rage. Arsène smiled.

'Come, sir, don't play a game with me! What! You take the precaution to bring me back alone in the van, you prepare a nice little block in the traffic, and you think that I am going to take to my heels and rejoin my friends! And what about the twenty detectives escorting us on foot, on bicycles, and in cabs? They'd have made short work of me: I should never have got off alive! Perhaps that was what they were reckoning on?'

Shrugging his shoulders, he added: 'I beg you sir, don't let them trouble about me. When I decide to escape I shall want nobody's assistance.'

Two days later the Echo de France, which was undoubtedly becoming the official gazette of the exploits of Arsène Lupin — he was said to be one of the principal shareholders — published the fullest details of his attempted escape. The exact text of the letters exchanged between the prisoner and his mysterious woman friend, the means employed for this correspondence, the part played by the police, the drive along the Boulevard Saint-Michel the incident at the Cafe Soufflot — everything was told in print. It was known that the inquiries of Inspector Dieuzy among the waiters of the restaurant had led to no result. And, in addition, the public were made aware of this bewildering fact, which showed the infinite variety of the resources which the man had at his disposal: the prison-van in which he had been carried was 'faked' from end to end, and had been substituted by his accomplices for one of the six regular vans that compose the prison service.

No one entertained any further doubt as to

Arsène Lupin's coming escape. He himself proclaimed it in categorical terms, as was shown by his reply to M. Bouvier on the day after the incident. The magistrate having bantered him on the check which he had encountered, he looked at him and said, coldly:

'Listen to me, sir, and take my word for it: this attempted escape formed part of my plan of escape.'

'I don't understand,' grinned the magistrate.

'There is no need that you should.'

And when, in the course of this private interrogatory, which appeared at full length in the columns of the Echo de France, the magistrate resumed his cross-examination, Lupin exclaimed, with a weary air:

'Oh dear, oh dear, oh dear! What is the use of going on? All these questions have no importance whatever.'

'How do you mean, no importance?'

'Of course not, seeing that I shall not attend my trial.'

'You will not attend? . . . '

'No, it's a fixed idea of mine, an irrevocable decision. Nothing will induce me to depart from it.'

This assurance, combined with the inexplicable indiscretions committed day after day, ended by enervating and disconcerting the officers of the law. Secrets were revealed, known to Arsène Lupin alone, the divulging of which could, therefore, come from none but him. But with what object did he divulge them? And by what means?

They changed Arsène Lupin's cell, moved him to a lower floor. The magistrate, on his side, closed the examination, and delivered the materials for the indictment.

A two months' silence ensued. These two months Arsène Lupin passed stretched on his bed, with his face almost constantly turned to the wall. The change of cell seemed to have crushed his spirits. He refused to see his counsel. He exchanged hardly a word with his wardens.

In the fortnight immediately preceding his trial he seemed to revive. He complained of lack of air. He was sent into the yard for exercise very early in the morning with a man on either side of him.

Meanwhile public curiosity had not abated. The news of his escape was expected daily; it was almost hoped for, so greatly had he caught the fancy of the crowd with his pluck, his gaiety, his variety, his inventive genius, and the mystery of his life. Arsène Lupin was bound to escape. It was inevitable. People were even astonished that he put it off so long. Every morning the prefect of police asked his secretary:

'Well, isn't he gone yet?'

'No, sir.'

'Then it will be to-morrow.'

And on the day before the trial a gentleman called at the office of the Grand Journal, asked to see the legal contributor, flung his card at his head, and made a rapid exit. The card bore the words:

Arsène Lupin always keeps his promises.

It was in these conditions that the trial opened. The crowd was enormous. Everybody wanted to see the famous Arsène Lupin, and was enjoying in advance the way in which he was sure to baffle the presiding judge. The court was thronged with barristers, magistrates, reporters, artists, society men and women — with all, in fact, that go to make up a first-night audience in Paris.

It was raining; the light was bad outside; it was difficult to see Arsène Lupin when his wardens ushered him into the dock. However, his torpid attitude, the manner in which he let himself fall into his chair, his indifferent and passive lack of movement, did not tell in his favour. His counsel — one of Maitre Danval's 'devils,' the great man himself having regarded the part to which he was reduced as beneath him — spoke to him several times. He jerked his head and made no reply.

The clerk of the court read the indictment. Then the presiding judge said:

'Prisoner at the bar, stand up. Give your name, your age, and your occupation.'

Receiving no answer, he repeated:

'Your name — what is your name?'

A thick and tired voice articulated the words:

'Desiré Baudru.'

There was a murmur in court. But the judge retorted:

'Desiré Baudru? Is this a new incarnation? As it is about the eighth name to which you lay claim, and no doubt as imaginary as the rest, we will keep, if you don't mind, to that of Arsène Lupin, under which you are more favourably known.'

The judge consulted his notes, and continued:

'For, notwithstanding all inquiries, it has been impossible to reconstruct your identity. You present the case, almost unparalleled in our modern society, of a man without a past. We do not know who you are, whence you come, where your childhood was spent — in short, we know nothing about you. You sprang up suddenly, three years ago, from an uncertain source, to reveal yourself as Arsène Lupin — that is to say, as a curious compound of intelligence and perversity, of criminality and generosity. The data which we have concerning you before that time are of the nature of suppositions. It seems probable that the so-called Rostat, who, eight years ago, was acting as assistant to Dickson, the conjurer, was none other than Arsène Lupin. It seems probable that the Russian student who, six years ago, used to attend Dr. Altier's laboratory at St. Louis' Hospital, and who often astonished the master by the ingenious character of his hypotheses on bacteriology and by the boldness of his experiments in the diseases of the skin — it seems probable that he too was none other than Arsène Lupin. So was the professor of Japanese wrestling, who established himself in Paris long before jiu-jitsu had been heard of. So, we believe, was the racing cyclist who won the great prize at the Exhibition, took his ten thousand francs, and has never been seen since. So, perhaps, was the man who saved so many people from burning at the Charity Bazaar, helping them through the little dormer window . . . and robbing them of their belongings.'

The judge paused for a moment, and concluded:

'Such was that period which seems to have been devoted entirely to a careful preparation for the struggle upon which you had embarked against society, a methodical apprenticeship in which you improved your force, your energy, and your skill to the highest pitch of perfection. Do you admit the accuracy of these facts?'

During this speech the defendant had shifted from foot to foot, with rounded back, and arms hanging slackly before him. As the light increased the spectators were able to distinguish his extreme emaciation, his sunken jaws, his curiously prominent cheek-bones, his earthen countenance, mottled with little red stains, and framed in a sparse and straggling beard. Prison had greatly aged and withered him. The clean-cut profile, the attractive, youthful features which had so often been reproduced in the papers, had passed away beyond all recognition.

He seemed not to have heard the question. It was twice repeated to him. At last he raised his eyes, appeared to think, and then, making a violent effort, muttered:

'Desiré Baudru.'

The judge laughed.

'I fail to follow exactly the system of

defence which you have adopted, Arsène Lupin. If it be to play the irresponsible imbecile, you must please yourself. As far as I am concerned, I shall go straight to the point without troubling about your fancies.'

And he enumerated in detail the robberies, swindles, and forgeries ascribed to Arsène Lupin. Occasionally he put a question to the prisoner. The latter gave a grunt or made no reply. Witness after witness entered the box. The evidence of several of them was insignificant; others delivered more important testimony; but all of them had one characteristic in common, which was that each contradicted the other. The trial was shrouded in a puzzling obscurity until Chief-Inspector Ganimard was called, when the general interest woke up.

Nevertheless, the old detective caused a certain disappointment from the first. He seemed not so much shy — he was too old a hand for that — as restless and ill at ease. He kept turning his eyes with visible embarrassment towards the prisoner. However, with his two hands resting on the ledge of the box, he described the incidents in which he had taken part, his pursuit of Lupin across Europe, his arrival in America. And the crowded court listened to him greedily, as it would have listened to the story of the most exciting adventures. But towards the close of his evidence, twice over, after alluding to his interviews with Arsène Lupin, he stopped with an absent and undecided air.

It was obvious that he was under the influence of some obsession. The judge said:

'If you are not feeling well, you can stand down and continue your evidence later.'

'No, no, only . . . '

He stopped, took a long and penetrating look at the prisoner, and said:

'Might I be allowed to see the prisoner more closely? There is a mystery which I want to clear up.'

He stepped across to the dock, gazed at the prisoner longer still, concentrating all his attention upon him, and returned to the witness-box. Then, in a solemn voice, he said:

'May it please the court, I swear that the man before me is not Arsène Lupin.'

A great silence greeted these words. The judge, at first taken aback, exclaimed:

'What do you mean? What are you saying? You are mad!'

The inspector declared, deliberately:

'At first sight one might be deceived by a likeness which, I admit, exists; but it needs only a momentary examination. The nose, the mouth, the hair, the colour of the skin: why, it's not Arsène Lupin at all. And look at the eyes: did he ever have those drunkard's eyes?'

'Come, come, explain yourself, witness. What do you mean?'

'I don't know. He must have substituted in his place and stead some poor wretch who would have been found guilty in his place and stead . . . unless this man is an accomplice.'

This unexpected denouement caused the greatest sensation in court. Cries of laughter and astonishment rose from every side. The judge gave instructions for the attendance of the examining magistrate, the governor of the Santé, and the warders — and suspended the sitting.

After the adjournment M. Bouvier and the governor, on being confronted with the prisoner, declared that there was only a very slight resemblance in features between the man and Arsène Lupin.

'But, in that case,' cried the judge, 'who is this man? Where does he come from? How does he come to be in the dock?'

The two warders from the Santé were called. To the general astonishment, they recognized the prisoner, whom it had been their business to watch by turns. The judge drew a breath.

But one of the warders went on to say:

'Yes, yes, I think it's the man.'

'What do you mean by saying you think?'

'Well, I hardly ever saw him. He was handed over to me at night, and for two months he was always lying on his bed with his face to the wall.'

'But before those two months?'

'Oh, before that, he was not in Cell 24.'

The governor of the prison explained:

'We changed his cell after his attempted escape.'

'But you, as governor, must have seen him since the last two months.'

'No, I had no occasion to see him . . . he kept quiet.'

'And this man is not the prisoner who was given into your keeping?'

'No.'

'Then who is he?'

'I don't know.'

'We have, therefore, to do with a substitution of personalities effected two months ago. How do you explain it?'

'I can't explain it.'

'Then . . .'

In despair the judge turned to the prisoner, and, in a coaxing voice, said:

'Prisoner, cannot you explain to me how and since when you come to be in the hands of the law?'

It seemed as though this benevolent tone disarmed the mistrust or stimulated the understanding of the man. He strove to reply. At last, skilfully and kindly questioned, he succeeded in putting together a few sentences which revealed that, two months before, he had been taken to the police-station and charged with vagrancy. He spent a night and a morning in the cells. Being found to possess a sum of seventy-five centimes, he was dismissed. But as he was crossing the yard two officers had caught him by the arm and taken him to the prison-van. Since that time he had been living in Cell 24 . . . He had been comfortable . . . Had had plenty to eat . . . Had slept pretty well . . . So he had not protested . . .

All this seemed probable. Amid laughter and a great effervescence of spirits the judge adjourned the case to another sitting for further inquiries.

The inquiries forthwith revealed the existence of an entry in the gaol-book to the effect that, eight weeks previously, a man of the name of Desiré Baudru had spent the night at the police-station. He was released the next day, and left the station at two o'clock in the afternoon. Well, at two o'clock on that day, Arsène Lupin, after undergoing his final examination, had left the police-station in the prison-van for the Santé.

Had the warders made a mistake? Had

they themselves, in an inattentive moment, deceived by the superficial likeness, substituted this man for their prisoner? This seemed hardly possible in view of the length of their service.

Had the substitution been planned in advance? Apart from the fact that the disposition localities made this almost unrealizable, it would have been necessary, in that case, that Baudru should be an accomplice, and cause himself to be arrested with the precise object of taking Arsène Lupin's place. But, then, by what miracle could a plan of this sort have succeeded, based, as it was, entirely on a series of improbable chances, of fortuitous meetings and fabulous mistakes?

Desiré Baudru was subjected to the anthropometrical test: there was not a single record corresponding with his description. Besides, traces of him were easily discovered. He was known at Courbevoie, at Asnieres, at Levallois. He lived by begging, and slept in one of those rag-pickers' huts of which there are so many near the Barriere Des Ternes. He had disappeared from sight for about a year.

Had he been suborned by Arsène Lupin? There were no grounds for thinking so. And even if this were so, it threw no light upon the prisoner's escape. The marvel remained as extraordinary as before. Of a score of suppositions put forward in explanation, not one was satisfactory. Of the escape alone there was no doubt: an incomprehensible, sensational escape, in which the public as well as the authorities felt the effect of a long preparation, a combination of wonderfully dove-tailed actions. And the upshot of it all was to justify Arsène Lupin's boastful prophecy:

'I shall not be present at my trial.'

After a month of careful investigations the puzzle continued to present the same inscrutable character. Still, it was impossible to keep that poor wretch of a Baudru indefinitely locked up. To try him would have been absurd — what charge was there against him? The magistrate signed the order for his release. But the head of the detective service resolved to keep an active supervision upon his movements.

The idea was suggested by Ganimard. In his opinion, there was an unconscious complicity and no accident in the matter. Baudru was an instrument that Arsène Lupin had employed with his amazing skill. With Baudru at large, they might hope, through him, to come upon Arsène Lupin, or, at least, upon one of his gang.

Inspectors Folenfant and Dieuzy were assigned as assistants to Ganimard, and one foggy morning in January the prison gates were thrown open to Desiré Baudru.

At first he seemed rather embarrassed, and walked like a man who has no very precise idea as to how to employ his time. He went down the Rue de la Santé and the Rue Saint-Jacques. Stopping outside an old-clothes shop, he took off his jacket and waistcoat, sold his waistcoat for a few sous, put on his jacket again, and went on.

He crossed the Seine. At the Chatelet an omnibus passed him. He tried to get into it. It was full. The ticket-collector advised him to take a number. He entered the waiting-room.

Ganimard beckoned to his two men, and, keeping his eyes on the office, said, quickly:

'Stop a cab . . . no, two cabs, that's better. I'll take one of you with me. We'll follow him.'

The men did as they were told. Baudru, however, did not appear. Ganimard went into the waiting-room: there was no one there.

'What a fool I am!' he muttered. 'I forgot the other door.'

The office, as a matter of fact, is connected with the other office in the Rue Saint-Martin. Ganimard rushed through the communicating passage. He was just in time to catch sight of Baudru on the top of the omnibus from Batignolles to the Jardin Des Plantes, which was turning the corner of the Rue de Rivoli.

He ran after the omnibus and caught it up. But he had lost his two assistants, and was continuing the pursuit alone.

In his rage he felt like taking Baudru by the collar without further form or ceremony. Was it not by premeditation and thanks to an ingenious trick that the so-called idiot had separated him from his two auxiliaries? He looked at Baudru. The man was dozing where he sat, and his head shook from right to left. His mouth was half open, his face wore an incredible expression of stupidity. No, this was not an adversary capable of taking old Ganimard in; chance had favoured him, that was all.

At the Carrefour Des Galeries-Lafayette, Baudru changed from the omnibus to the La Muette tram-car. Ganimard followed his example. They went along the Boulevard Haussmann and the Avenue Victor-Hugo. Baudru alighted at the stopping-place at La Muette, and, with a lounging step, entered the Bois de Boulogne.

He passed from one alley to another, retraced his steps, and went on again. What was he looking for? Had he an object in view?

After an hour of these manoeuvres he seemed tired and worn out. Catching sight of a bench, he sat down upon it. The spot was not far from Auteuil, on the brink of a little lake hidden among the trees, and was absolutely deserted. Half an hour elapsed. At last, losing patience, Ganimard resolved to enter into conversation.

He therefore went up and took a seat by Baudru's side. He lit a cigarette, drew a pattern in the sand with the end of his walking-stick, and said:

'A cold day.'

Silence. And suddenly in this silence a peal of laughter rang out — a peal of glad and happy laughter, the laughter of a child seized with a fit of laughter, and utterly unable to keep from laughing, laughing, laughing. Ganimard felt his hair literally and positively stand on end on his head. That laugh, that infernal laugh, which he knew so well! . . .

With an abrupt movement he caught the man by the lapels of his jacket, and gave him a violent and penetrating look — looked at him even more closely than he had done at the criminal court; and, in truth, it was no longer the man he had seen. It was the man, but, at the same time, it was the other, the real man.

Aided by the wish which is father to the thought, he rediscovered the glowing light in the eyes, he filled in the sunken features, he saw the real flesh under the wizened skin, the real mouth through the grimace which deformed it. And it was the other's eyes, it was the other's mouth, it was — it was, above all — his keen, lively, mocking, witty expression, so bright and so young.

'Arsène Lupin! Arsène Lupin!' he stammered.

And in a sudden access of rage he caught him by the throat and tried to throw him down. Notwithstanding his fifty years, he was still a man of uncommon vigor, whereas his adversary seemed quite out of condition. And what a master-stroke it would be if he succeeded in bringing him back!

The struggle was short. Arsène Lupin hardly made a movement in defence and Ganimard let go as promptly as he had attacked. His right arm hung numbed and lifeless by his side.

'If they taught you jiu-jitsu at the Quai Des Orfevres,' said Lupin, 'you would know that they call this movement uli-shi-ghi in Japanese.' And he added, coldly: 'Another second and I should have broken your arm, and you would have had no more than you deserve. What! You, an old friend, whom I esteem, before whom I reveal my incognito of my own accord, would you abuse my confidence? It's very wrong of you! . . . Hullo, what's the matter now?'

Ganimard was silent. This escape, for

which he held himself responsible — was it not he who, by his sensational evidence, had diverted the ends of justice? — this escape seemed to him to mark the disgrace of his career. A tear trickled slowly down his cheek towards his grey moustache.

'Why, goodness me, Ganimard, don't take on like that! If you hadn't spoken I should have arranged for some one else to speak. Come, come, how could I have allowed them to find a verdict against Desiré Baudru?'

'So it was you that were there?' muttered Ganimard. 'And it is you that are here?'

'Yes, I, I, no one but me.'

'Is it possible?'

'Oh, one needn't be a wizard for that. It is enough, as that worthy judge said, to prepare one's self for a dozen years or so in order to be ready for every eventuality.'

'But your face? Your eyes?'

'You can understand that when I worked for eighteen months at St. Louis' with Dr. Altier it was not for love of art. I felt that the man who would one day have the honour of calling himself Arsène Lupin ought to be exempt from the ordinary laws of personal appearance and identity. You can modify your appearance as you please. A hypodermic injection of paraffin puffs up your skin to just the extent desired. Pyrogallic acid turns you into a Cherokee Indian. Celandine juice adorns you with blotches and pimples of the most pleasing kind. A certain chemical process affects the growth of your hair and beard, another the sound of your voice. Add to that, two months of dieting in Cell 24, incessant practice, at opening my mouth with this particular grimace and carrying my head at this angle and my back at this stoop. Lastly, five drops of atropine in the eyes to make them haggard and dilated, and the trick is done!'

'I can't see how the warders . . . '

'The change was slow and progressive. They could never have noticed its daily evolution.'

'But Desiré Baudru . . . ?'

'Baudru is a real person. He is a poor, harmless beggar whom I met last year, and whose features are really not quite unlike my own. Foreseeing an always possible arrest, I placed him in safe-keeping, and applied myself from the first to picking out the points of dissimilarity between us, so as to diminish these in myself as far as I could. My friends made him pass a night at the police-station in such a way that he left it at about the same time as I did and the coincidence could be easily established. For, observe, it was necessary that his passage

90

should be traceable, else the lawyers would have wanted to know who I was; whereas, by offering them that excellent Baudru I made it inevitable — do you follow me? — inevitable that they should jump at him, in spite of the insurmountable difficulties of a substitution — prefer to believe in that substitution rather than admit their ignorance.'

'Yes, yes, that's true,' muttered Ganimard.

'And then,' cried Arsène Lupin, 'I held a formidable trump in my hand, a card which I had prepared from the start: the universal expectation of my escape! And there you see the clumsy mistake into which you and all of you fell in this exciting game which the law and I were playing, with my liberty for the stakes: you again thought that I was bragging, that I was intoxicated with my successes, like the veriest greenhorn! Fancy me, Arsène Lupin, guilty of such weakness! And, just as in the Cahorn case, you failed to say to yourselves: 'As soon as Arsène Lupin proclaims from the house-tops that he means to escape he must have some reason that obliges him to proclaim it.' But, hang it all, don't you see that, in order to escape . . . without escaping, it was essential that people should believe beforehand in my escape, that it should be an article of faith, an absolute conviction, a truth clear as daylight? And that is what it became, in accordance with my will. Arsène Lupin intended to escape, Arsène Lupin did not intend to be present at his trial. And when you stood up and said, 'That man is not Arsène Lupin,' it would have been beyond human nature for all those present not at once to believe that I was not Arsène Lupin. Had only one person expressed a doubt, had only one person uttered this simple reservation, 'But suppose it is Arsène Lupin?' . . . that very moment I should have been lost. They had only to bend over and look at me, not with the idea that I was not Arsène Lupin, as you and the rest did, but with the idea that I might be Arsène Lupin, and, in spite of all my precautions, I should have been recognized. But I was quite easy in my mind. It was logically and psychologically impossible for anybody to have that simple little idea.'

He suddenly seized Ganimard's hand.

'Look here, Ganimard, confess that, a week after our interview at the Santé prison, you stayed in for me, at four o'clock, as I asked you to?'

'And your prison-van?' said Ganimard, evading the question.

'Bluff, mere bluff. My friends had faked up that old discarded van and substituted it for the other, and they wanted to try the experiment. But I knew that it was impracticable without the co-operation of exceptional circumstances. Only I thought it useful to complete this attempted escape and to give it the proper publicity. A first escape, boldly planned, gave to the second the full value of an escape realized in advance.'

'So the cigar . . . '

'Was scooped out by myself; and the knife, too.'

'And the notes?'

'Written by me.'

'And the mysterious correspondent?'

'She and I were one. I can write any hand I please.'

Ganimard thought for a moment, and said:

'How was it that, when they took Baudru's measurements in the anthropometrical room, these were not found to coincide with the record of Arsène Lupin?'

'Arsène Lupin's record does not exist.'

'Nonsense!'

'Or, at least, it is not correct. This is a question to which I have devoted a good deal of study. The Bertillon system allows for, first, a visual description — and you have seen that this is not infallible — and, next, a description by measurements: measurements of the head, the fingers, the ears, and so on. There is nothing to be done against that.'

'So? . . .'

'So I had to pay. Before my return from America one of the clerks of the staff accepted a definite bribe to enter one false measurement at the start. This is enough to throw the whole system out of gear, and to cause a record to stray into a compartment diametrically opposite to the compartment in which it ought to go. The Baudru record could not, therefore, possibly agree with the Arsène Lupin record.'

There was another silence, and then Ganimard asked:

'And what are you going to do now?'

'Now!' exclaimed Lupin. 'I am going to take a rest, feed myself up and gradually become myself again. It's all very well to be Baudru or another, to change your personality as you would your boots, and to select your appearance, your voice, your expression, your handwriting. But there comes a time when you cease to know yourself amid all these changes, and that is very sad. I feel at present as the man must have felt who lost his shadow. I am going to look for myself . . . and to find myself.'

He walked up and down. The daylight was waning. He stopped in front of Ganimard.

'We've said all that we had to say to each other, I suppose?'

'No,' replied the inspector. 'I should like to know if you intend to publish the truth about your escape . . . and the mistake I made . . . '

'Oh, no one will ever know that it was Arsène Lupin that was released. I have too great an interest to serve in heaping up the most mysterious darkness around me, and I should not dream of depriving my flight of its almost miraculous character. So have no fear, my dear friend; and good-bye. I am dining out to-night, and have only just time to dress.'

'I thought you were so anxious for a rest.'

'Alas, there are social engagements from which it is impossible to escape. My rest must begin tomorrow'

'And where are you dining, may I ask?'

'At the British Embassy.'

The Mysterious Traveller

I had sent my motor-car to Rouen by road on the previous day I was to meet it by train, and go on to some friends, who have a house on the Seine.

A few minutes before we left Paris my compartment was invaded by seven gentlemen, five of whom were smoking. Short though the journey by the fast train be, I did not relish the prospect of taking it in such company, the more so as the old-fashioned carriage had no corridor. I therefore collected my overcoat, my newspapers, and my railway guide, and sought refuge in one of the neighbouring compartments.

It was occupied by a lady. At the sight of me, she made a movement of vexation which did not escape my notice, and leaned towards a gentleman standing on the foot-board — her husband, no doubt, who had come to see her off. The gentleman took stock of me, and the examination seemed to conclude to my advantage; for he whispered to his wife and smiled, giving her the look with which we reassure a frightened child. She smiled in her turn, and cast a friendly glance in my direction, as though she suddenly realized that I was one of those well-bred men with whom a woman can remain locked up for an hour or two in a little box six feet square without having anything to fear.

Her husband said to her:

'You must not mind, darling; but I have an important appointment, and I must not wait.'

He kissed her affectionately, and went away. His wife blew him some discreet little kisses through the window, and waved her handkerchief.

Then the guard's whistle sounded, and the train started.

At that moment, and in spite of the warning shouts of the railway officials, the door opened, and a man burst into our carriage. My travelling companion, who was standing up and arranging her things in the rack, uttered a cry of terror, and dropped down upon the seat.

I am no coward — far from it; but I confess that these sudden incursions at the last minute are always annoying. They seem so ambiguous, so unnatural. There must be something behind them, else . . .

The appearance of the newcomer, however, and his bearing were such as to correct the bad impression produced by the manner of his entrance. He was neatly, almost smartly, dressed; his tie was in good taste, his gloves clean; he had a powerful face ... But, speaking of his face, where on earth had I seen it before? For I had seen it: of that there was no possible doubt; or at least, to be accurate, I found within myself that sort of recollection which is left by the sight of an oft-seen portrait of which one has never beheld the original. And at the same time I felt the uselessness of any effort of memory that I might exert, so inconsistent and vague was that recollection.

But when my eyes reverted to the lady I sat astounded at the pallor and disorder of her features. She was staring at her neighbour — he was seated on the same side of the carriage — with an expression of genuine affright, and I saw one of her hands steal trembling towards a little travelling-bag that lay on the cushion a few inches from her lap. She ended by taking hold of it, and nervously drew it to her.

Our eyes met, and I read in hers so great an amount of uneasiness and anxiety that I could not help saying:

'I hope you are not unwell, madame ... Would you like me to open the window?'

She made no reply, but, with a timid gesture, called my attention to the individual beside her. I smiled as her husband had done, shrugged my shoulders, and explained to her by signs that she had nothing to fear, that I was there, and that, besides, the gentleman in question seemed quite harmless.

Just then he turned towards us, contemplated us, one after the other, from head to foot, and then huddled himself into his corner, and made no further movement.

A silence ensued; but the lady, as though she had summoned up all her energies to perform an act of despair, said to me, in a hardly audible voice:

'You know he is in our train.'

'Who?'

'Why, he . . . he himself . . . I assure you.'

'Whom do you mean?'

'Arsène Lupin!'

She had not removed her eyes from the passenger, and it was at him rather than at me that she flung the syllables of that alarming name.

He pulled his hat down upon his nose. Was this to conceal his agitation, or was he merely preparing to go to sleep?

I objected.

'Arsène Lupin was sentenced yesterday, in his absence, to twenty years' penal servitude. It is not likely that he would commit the imprudence of showing himself in public to-day. Besides, the newspapers have discovered that he has been spending the winter in Turkey ever since his famous escape from the Santé.'

'He is in this train,' repeated the lady, with the ever more marked intention of being overheard by our companion. 'My husband is a deputy prison-governor, and the station-inspector himself told us that they were looking for Arsène Lupin.'

'That is no reason why . . . '

'He was seen at the booking-office. He took a ticket for Rouen.'

'It would have been easy to lay hands upon him.'

'He disappeared. The ticket-collector at the door of the waiting-room did not see him; but they thought that he must have gone round by the suburban platforms and stepped into the express that leaves ten minutes after us.'

'In that case, they will have caught him there.'

'And supposing that, at the last moment, he jumped out of that express and entered this, our own train . . . as he probably . . . as he most certainly did?'

'In that case they will catch him here; for the porters and the police cannot have failed to see him going from one train to the other, and, when we reach Rouen, they will net him finely.'

'Him? Never! He will find some means of escaping again.'

'In that case I wish him a good journey.'

'But think of all that he may do in the mean time!'

'What?'

'How can I tell? One must be prepared for anything.'

She was greatly agitated; and, in point of fact, the situation, to a certain degree, warranted her nervous state of excitement. Almost in spite of myself, I said:

'There are such things as curious coincidences, it is true ... But calm yourself. Admitting that Arsène Lupin is in one of these carriages, he is sure to keep quiet, and, rather than bring fresh trouble upon himself, he will have no other idea than that of avoiding the danger that threatens him.'

My words failed to reassure her. However she said no more, fearing, no doubt, lest I should think her troublesome.

As for myself, I opened my newspapers and read the reports of Arsène Lupin's trial. They contained nothing that was not already known, and they interested me but slightly. Moreover, I was tired, I had had a poor night, I felt my eye-lids growing heavy, and my head began to nod.

'But surely, sir, you are not going to sleep?'

The lady snatched my paper from my hands, and looked at me with indignation.

'Certainly not,' I replied. 'I have no wish to.'

'It would be most imprudent,' she said.

'Most,' I repeated.

And I struggled hard, fixing my eyes on the landscape, on the clouds that streaked the sky. And soon all this became confused in space, the image of the excited lady and the drowsy man was obliterated in my mind, and I was filled with the great, deep silence of sleep.

It was soon made agreeable by light and incoherent dreams, in which a being who played the part and bore the name of Arsène Lupin occupied a certain place. He turned and shifted on the horizon, his back laden with valuables, clambering over walls and stripping country-houses of their contents.

But the outline of this being, who had ceased to be Arsène Lupin, grew more distinct. He came towards me, grew bigger and bigger, leaped into the carriage with incredible agility, and fell full upon my chest.

A sharp pain . . . a piercing scream . . . I

awoke. The man, my fellow-traveler, with one knee on my chest, was clutching my throat.

I saw this very dimly, for my eyes were shot with blood. I also saw the lady in a corner writhing in a violent fit of hysterics. I did not even attempt to resist. I should not have had the strength for it had I wished to: my temples were throbbing, I choked ... my throat rattled ... Another minute ... and I should have been suffocated.

The man must have felt this. He loosened his grip. Without leaving hold of me, with his right hand he stretched a rope, in which he had prepared a slipknot, and, with a quick turn, tied my wrists together. In a moment I was bound, gagged — rendered motionless and helpless.

And he performed this task in the most natural manner in the world, with an ease that revealed the knowledge of a master, of an expert in theft and crime. Not a word, not a fevered movement. Sheer coolness and audacity. And there lay I on the seat, roped up like a mummy — I, Arsène Lupin!

It was really ridiculous. And notwithstanding the seriousness of the circumstances I could not but appreciate and almost enjoy the irony of the situation. Arsène Lupin 'done' like a novice, stripped like the first-comer! For of course the scoundrel relieved me of my pocket-book and purse! Arsène Lupin victimized in his turn — duped and beaten! What an adventure!

There remained the lady. He took no notice of her at all. He contented himself with picking up the wrist-bag that lay on the floor, and extracting the jewels, the purse, the gold and silver knick-knacks which it contained. The lady opened her eyes, shuddered with fright, took off her rings and handed them to the man as though she wished to spare him any superfluous exertion. He took the rings, and looked at her: she fainted away.

Then, calm and silent as before, without troubling about us further, he resumed his seat, lit a cigarette, and abandoned himself to a careful scrutiny of the treasures which he had captured, the inspection of which seemed to satisfy him completely.

I was much less satisfied. I am not speaking of the twelve thousand francs of which I had been unduly plundered: this was a loss which I accepted only for the time; I had no doubt that those twelve thousand francs would return to my possession after a short interval, together with the exceedingly important papers which my pocketbook contained: plans, estimates, specifications, addresses, lists of correspondents, letters of a coin-promising character. But, for the moment, a more immediate and serious care was worrying me: what was to happen next?

As may be readily imagined, the excitement caused by my passing through the Gare Saint-Lazare had not escaped me. As I was going to stay with friends who knew me by the name of Guillaume Berlat, and to whom my resemblance to Arsène Lupin was the occasion of many a friendly jest, I had not been able to disguise myself after my wont, and my presence had been discovered. Moreover, a man, doubtless Arsène Lupin, had been seen to rush from the express into the fast train. Hence it was inevitable and fated that the commissary of police at Rouen, warned by telegram, would await the arrival of the train, assisted by a respectable number of constables, question any suspicious passengers, and proceed to make a minute inspection of the carriages.

All this I had foreseen, and had not felt greatly excited about it; for I was certain that the Rouen police would display no greater perspicacity than the Paris police, and that I should have been able to pass unperceived: was it not sufficient for me, at the wicket, carelessly to show my deputy's card, collector at Saint-Lazare with every confidence? But how things had changed since then! I was no longer free. It was impossible to attempt one

105

of my usual moves. In one of the carriages the commissary would discover the Sieur Arsène Lupin, whom a propitious fate was sending to him bound hand and foot, gentle as a lamb, packed up complete. He had only to accept delivery, just as you receive a parcel addressed to you at a railway station, a hamper of game, or a basket of vegetables and fruit.

And to avoid this annoying catastrophe, what could I do, entangled as I was in my bonds?

And the train was speeding towards Rouen, the next and the only stopping-place; it rushed through Vernon, through Saint-Pierre . . .

I was puzzled also by another problem in which I was not so directly interested, but the solution of which aroused my professional curiosity: What were my fellow-traveller's intentions?

If I had been alone he would have had ample time to alight quite calmly at Rouen. But the lady? As soon as the carriage door was opened the lady, meek and quiet as she sat at present, would scream, and throw herself about, and cry for help!

Hence my astonishment. Why did he not reduce her to the same state of powerlessness as myself, which would have given him time to disappear before his twofold misdeed was discovered?

He was still smoking, his eyes fixed on the view outside, which a hesitating rain was beginning to streak with long, slanting lines. Once, however, he turned round, took up my railway guide, and consulted it.

As for the lady, she made every effort to continue fainting, so as to quiet her enemy. But a fit of coughing, produced by the smoke, gave the lie to her pretended swoon.

Myself, I was very uncomfortable, and had pains all over my body. And I thought . . . I planned.

Pont-de-l'Arche . . . Oissel . . . The train was hurrying on, glad, drunk with speed . . . Saint-Etienne . . .

At that moment the man rose and took two steps towards us, to which the lady hastened to reply with a new scream and a genuine fainting fit.

But what could his object be? He lowered the window on our side. The rain was now falling in torrents, and he made a movement of annoyance at having neither umbrella nor overcoat. He looked up at the rack: the lady's en-tout-cas was there; he took it. He also took my overcoat and put it on.

We were crossing the Seine. He turned up his trousers, and then, leaning out of the window, raised the outer latch.

Did he mean to fling himself on the

permanent way? At the rate at which we were going it would have been certain death. We plunged into the tunnel pierced under the Cote Sainte-Catherine. The man opened the door, and, with one foot, felt for the step. What madness! The darkness, the smoke, the din — all combined to give a fantastic appearance to any such attempt. But suddenly the train slowed up, the Westinghouse brakes counteracted the movement of the wheels. In a minute the pace from fast became normal, and decreased still more. Without a doubt there was a gang at work repairing this part of the tunnel; this would necessitate a slower passage of the trains for some days perhaps, and the man knew it.

He had only, therefore, to put his other foot on the step, climb down to the footboard, and walk away quietly, not without first closing the door, and throwing back the latch.

He had scarcely disappeared when the smoke showed whiter in the daylight. We emerged into a valley. One more tunnel, and we should be at Rouen.

The lady at once recovered her wits, and her first care was to bewail the loss of her jewels. I gave her a beseeching glance. She understood, and relieved me of the gag which was stifling me. She wanted also to unfasten my bonds, but I stopped her.

'No, no; the police must see everything as it was. I want them to be fully informed as regards that blackguard's actions.'

'Shall I pull the alarm-signal?'

'Too late. You should have thought of that while he was attacking me.'

'But he would have killed me! Ah, sir, didn't I tell you that he was travelling by this train? I knew him at once, by his portrait. And now he's taken my jewels!'

'They'll catch him, have no fear.'

'Catch Arsène Lupin! Never.'

'It all depends on you, madam. Listen. When we arrive be at the window, call out, make a noise. The police and porters will come up. Tell them what you have seen in a few words: the assault of which I was the victim, and the flight of Arsène Lupin. Give his description: a soft hat, an umbrella — yours — a grey frock-overcoat . . . '

'Yours,' she said.

'Mine? No, his own. I didn't have one.'

'I thought that he had none either when he got in.'

'He must have had . . . unless it was a coat which some one left behind in the rack. In any case, he had it when he got out, and that is the essential thing . . . A grey frock-overcoat, remember . . . Oh, I was forgetting

. . . tell them your name to start with. Your husband's functions will stimulate the zeal of all those men.'

We were arriving. She was already leaning out of the window. I resumed, in a louder, almost imperious voice, so that my words should sink into her brain:

'Give my name also, Guillaume Berlat. If necessary, say you know me . . . That will save time . . . we must hurry on the preliminary inquiries . . . the important thing is to catch Arsène Lupin . . . with your jewels . . . You quite understand, don't you? Guillaume Berlat, a friend of your husband's.'

'Quite . . . Guillaume Berlat.'

She was already calling out and gesticulating. Before the train had come to a standstill a gentleman climbed in, followed by a number of other men. The critical hour was at hand.

Breathlessly the lady exclaimed:

'Arsène Lupin . . . he attacked us . . . he has stolen my jewels . . . I am Madame Renaud . . . my husband is a deputy prison-governor . . . Ah, here's my brother, Georges Andelle, manager of the Credit Rouennais . . . What I want to say is . . . '

She kissed a young man who had just come up, and who exchanged greetings with the commissary. She continued, weeping:

'Yes, Arsène Lupin . . . He flew at this gentleman's throat in his sleep . . . Monsieur Berlat, a friend of my husband's.'

'But where is Arsène Lupin?'

'He jumped out of the train in the tunnel, after we had crossed the Seine.'

'Are you sure it was he?'

'Certain. I recognized him at once. Besides, he was seen at the Gare Saint-Lazare. He was wearing a soft hat . . . '

'No; a hard felt hat, like this,' said the commissary, pointing to my hat.

'A soft hat, I assure you,' repeated Madame Renaud, 'and a grey frock-overcoat.'

'Yes,' muttered the commissary; 'the telegram mentions a grey frock-overcoat with a black velvet collar.'

'A black velvet collar, that's it!' exclaimed Madame Renaud, triumphantly.

I breathed again. What a good, excellent friend I had found in her!

Meanwhile the policemen had released me from my bonds. I bit my lips violently till the blood flowed. Bent in two, with my handkerchief to my mouth, as seems proper to a man who has long been sitting in a constrained position, and who bears on his face the blood-stained marks of the gag, I said to the commissary, in a feeble voice:

'Sir, it was Arsène Lupin, there is no doubt

of it . . . You can catch him if you hurry . . . I think I may be of some use to you . . . '

The coach, which was needed for the inspection by the police, was slipped. The remainder of the train went on towards Le Havre. We were taken to the station-master's office through a crowd of on-lookers who filled the platform.

Just then I felt a hesitation. I must make some excuse to absent myself, find my motorcar, and be off. It was dangerous to wait. If anything happened, if a telegram came from Paris, I was lost.

Yes; but what about my robber? Left to my own resources, in a district with which I was not very well acquainted, I could never hope to come up with him.

'Bah!' I said to myself. 'Let us risk it, and stay. It's a difficult hand to win, but a very amusing one to play. And the stakes are worth the trouble.'

And as we were being asked provisionally to repeat our depositions, I exclaimed:

'Mr. Commissary, Arsène Lupin is getting a start of us. My motor is waiting for me in the yard. If you will do me the pleasure to accept a seat in it, we will try . . . '

The commissary gave a knowing smile.

'It's not a bad idea . . . such a good idea, in fact, that it's already being carried out.'

'Oh!'

'Yes; two of my officers started on bicycles . . . some time ago.'

'But where to?'

'To the entrance to the tunnel. There they will pick up the clues and the evidence, and follow the track of Arsène Lupin.'

I could not help shrugging my shoulders.

'Your two officers will pick up no clues and no evidence.'

'Really!'

'Arsène Lupin will have arranged that no one should see him leave the tunnel. He will have taken the nearest road, and from there . . . '

'From there made for Rouen, where we shall catch him.'

'He will not go to Rouen.'

'In that case, he will remain in the neighbourhood, where we shall be even more certain . . . '

'He will not remain in the neighbourhood.'

'Oh! Then where will he hide himself?'

I took out my watch.

'At this moment Arsène Lupin is hanging about the station at Darnetal. At ten-fifty — that is to say, in twenty-two minutes from now — he will take the train which leaves Rouen from the Gare du Nord for Amiens.'

'Do you think so? And how do you know?'

'Oh, it's very simple. In the carriage Arsène Lupin consulted my railway guide. What for? To see if there was another line near the place where he disappeared, a station on that line, and a train which stopped at that station. I have just looked at the guide myself, and learned what I wanted to know.'

'Upon my word, sir,' said the commissary, 'you possess marvellous powers of deduction. What an expert you must be!'

Dragged on by my certainty, I had blundered by displaying too much cleverness. He looked at me in astonishment, and I saw that a suspicion flickered through his mind. Only just, it is true; for the photographs dispatched in every direction were so unlike, represented an Arsène Lupin so different from the one that stood before him, that he could not possibly recognize the original in me. Nevertheless, he was troubled, restless, perplexed.

There was a moment of silence. A certain ambiguity and doubt seemed to interrupt our words. A shudder of anxiety passed through me.

Was luck about to turn against me? Mastering myself, I began to laugh.

'Ah well, there's nothing to sharpen one's wits like the loss of a pocketbook and the desire to find it again. And it seems to me that, if you will give me two of your men, the three of us might, perhaps . . . '

'Oh, please, Mr. Commissary,' exclaimed Madame Renaud, 'do what Monsieur Berlat suggests.'

My kind friend's intervention turned the scale. Uttered by her, the wife of an influential person, the name of Berlat became mine in reality, and conferred upon me an identity which no suspicion could touch. The commissary rose.

'Believe me, Monsieur Berlat, I shall be only too pleased to see you succeed. I am as anxious as yourself to have Arsène Lupin arrested.'

He accompanied me to my car. He introduced two of his men to me: Honoré Massol and Gaston Delivet. They took their seats. I placed myself at the wheel. My chauffeur started the engine. A few seconds later we had left the station. I was saved.

I confess that as we dashed in my powerful 35-h.p. Moreau-Lepton along the boulevards that skirt the old Norman city I was not without a certain sense of pride. The engine hummed harmoniously. The trees sped behind us to right and left. And now, free and out of danger, I had nothing to do but to settle my own little private affairs with the co-operation of two worthy representatives of the law. Arsène Lupin was going in search of Arsène Lupin!

Ye humble mainstays of the social order of things, Gaston Delivet and Honoré Massol, how precious was your assistance to me! Where should I have been without you? But for you, at how many cross-roads should I have taken the wrong turning! But for you, Arsène Lupin would have gone astray and the other escaped!

But all was not over yet. Far from it. I had first to capture the fellow and next to take possession, myself, of the papers of which he had robbed me. At no cost must my two satellites be allowed to catch a sight of those documents, much less lay hands upon them. To make use of them and yet act independently of them was what I wanted to do; and it was no easy matter.

We reached Darnetal three minutes after the train had left. I had the consolation of learning that a man in a grey frock-overcoat with a black velvet collar had got into a second-class carriage with a ticket for Amiens. There was no doubt about it: my first appearance as a detective was a promising one.

Delivet said:

'The train is an express, and does not stop before Monterolier-Buchy, in nineteen minutes from now. If we are not there before

Arsène Lupin he can go on towards Amiens, branch off to Cleres, and, from there, make for Dieppe or Paris.'

'How far is Monterolier?'

'Fourteen miles and a half.'

'Fourteen miles and a half in nineteen minutes . . . We shall be there ahead of him.'

It was a stirring race. Never had my trusty Moreau-Lepton responded to my impatience with greater ardour and regularity. It seemed to me as though I communicated my wishes to her directly, without the intermediary of levers or handles. She shared my desires. She approved of my determination. She understood my animosity against that blackguard Arsène Lupin. The scoundrel! The sneak! Should I get the best of him? Or would he once more baffle authority, that authority of which I was the incarnation?

'Right!' cried Delivet . . . 'Left! . . . Straight ahead! . . . '

We skimmed the ground. The mile-stones looked like little timid animals that fled at our approach.

And suddenly at the turn of a road a cloud of smoke — the north express!

For half a mile it was a struggle side by side — an unequal struggle, of which the issue was certain — we beat the train by twenty lengths.

In three seconds we were on the platform in front of the second class. The doors were flung open. A few people stepped out. My thief was not among them. We examined the carriages. No Arsène Lupin.

'By Jove!' I exclaimed, 'he must have recognized me in the motor while we were going alongside of him, and jumped!'

The guard of the train confirmed my supposition. He had seen a man scrambling down the embankment at two hundred yards from the station.

'There he is! . . . Look! . . . At the level crossing!'

I darted in pursuit, followed by my two satellites, or, rather, by one of them; for the other, Massol, turned out to be an uncommonly fast sprinter, gifted with both speed and staying power. In a few seconds the distance between him and the fugitive was greatly diminished. The man saw him, jumped a hedge, and scampered off towards a slope, which he climbed. We saw him, farther still, entering a little wood.

When we reached the wood we found Massol waiting for us. He had thought it no use to go on, lest he should lose us.

'You were quite right, my dear fellow,' I said. 'After a run like this our friend must be exhausted. We've got him.'

I examined the skirts of the wood while thinking how I could best proceed alone to arrest the fugitive, in order myself to effect certain recoveries which the law, no doubt, would only have allowed after a number of disagreeable inquiries. Then I returned to my companions.

'Look here, it's very easy. You, Massol, take up your position on the left. You, Delivet, on the right. From there you can watch the whole rear of the wood, and he can't leave it unseen by you except by this hollow, where I shall stand. If he does not come out, I'll go in and force him back towards one or the other of you. You have nothing to do, therefore, but wait. Oh, I was forgetting: in case of alarm, I'll fire a shot.'

Massol and Delivet moved off, each to his own side. As soon as they were out of sight I made my way into the wood with infinite precautions, so as to be neither seen nor heard. It consisted of close thickets, contrived for the shooting, and intersected by very narrow paths, in which it was only possible to walk by stooping, as though in a leafy tunnel.

One of these ended in a glade, where the damp grass showed the marks of footsteps. I followed them, taking care to steal through the underwood. They led me to the bottom of a little mound, crowned by a tumble-down

119

lath-and-plaster hovel.

'He must be there,' I thought. 'He has selected a good post of observation.'

I crawled close up to the building. A slight sound warned me of his presence, and, in fact, I caught sight of him through an opening; with his back turned towards me.

Two bounds brought me upon him. He tried to point the revolver which he held in his hand. I did not give him time, but pulled him to the ground in such a way that his two arms were twisted and caught under him, while I held him pinned down with my knee upon his chest.

'Listen to me, old chap,' I whispered in his ear. 'I am Arsène Lupin. You've got to give me back, this minute and without any fuss, my pocketbook and the lady's wrist-bag . . . in return for which I'll save you from the clutches of the police and enroll you among my friends. Which is it to be: yes or no?'

'Yes,' he muttered.

'That's right. Your plan of this morning was cleverly thought out. We shall be good friends.'

I got up. He fumbled in his pocket, fetched out a great knife, and tried to strike me with it.

'Imbecile!' I cried.

With one hand I parried the attack. With

the other I caught him a violent blow on the carotid artery, the blow which is known as 'the carotid hook.' He fell back stunned.

In my pocketbook I found my papers and bank-notes. I took his own out of curiosity. On an envelope addressed to him I read his name: Pierre Onfrey.

I gave a start. Pierre Onfrey, the perpetrator of the murder in the Rue Lafontaine at Auteuil! Pierre Onfrey, the man who had cut the throats of Madame Delbois and her two daughters. I bent over him. Yes, that was the face which, in the railway-carriage, had aroused in me the memory of features which I had seen before.

But time was passing. I placed two hundred-franc notes in an envelope, with a visiting-card bearing these words:

'Arsène Lupin to his worthy assistants, Honoré Massol and Gaston Delivet, with his best thanks.'

I laid this where it could be seen, in the middle of the room. Beside it I placed Madame Renaud's wrist-bag. Why should it not be restored to the kind friend who had rescued me? I confess, however, that I took from it everything that seemed in any way interesting, leaving only a tortoise-shell comb, a stick of lip-salve, and an empty purse. Business is business, when all is said and done! And, besides, her husband followed such a disreputable occupation! . . .

There remained the man. He was beginning to move. What was I to do? I was not qualified either to save or to condemn him.

I took away his weapons, and fired my revolver in the air.

'That will bring the two others,' I thought. 'He must find a way out of his own difficulties. Let fate take its course.'

And I went down the hollow road at a run.

Twenty minutes later a cross-road which I had noticed during our pursuit brought me back to my car.

At four o'clock I telegraphed to my friends from Rouen that an unexpected incident compelled me to put off my visit. Between ourselves, I greatly fear that, in view of what they must now have learned, I shall be obliged to postpone it indefinitely. It will be a cruel disappointment for them!

At six o'clock I returned to Paris by L'Isle-Adam, Enghien, and the Porte Bineau.

I gathered from the evening papers that the police had at last succeeded in capturing Pierre Onfrey.

The next morning — why should we despise the advantages of intelligent advertisement? — the Echo de France contained the following sensational paragraph:

'Yesterday, near Buchy, after a number of incidents, Arsène Lupin effected the arrest of Pierre Onfrey. The Auteuil murderer had robbed a lady of the name of Renaud, the wife of the deputy prison-governor, in the train between Paris and Le Havre. Arsène Lupin has restored to Madame Renaud the wrist-bag which contained her jewels, and has generously rewarded the two detectives who assisted him in the matter of this dramatic arrest.'

The Queen's Necklace

Two or three times a year, on the occasion of important functions, such as the balls at the Austrian Embassy or Lady Billingstone's receptions, the Comtesse de Dreux-Soubise would wear the Queen's Necklace.

This was really the famous necklace, the historic necklace, which Böhmer and Bassange, the crown jewellers, had designed for the Du Barry, which the Cardinal de Rohan-Soubise believed himself to be presenting to the Queen Marie-Antoinette, and which Jeanne de Valois, Comtesse de La Motte, the adventuress, took to pieces, one evening in February, 1785, with the assistance of her husband and their accomplice, Rétaux de Villette.

As a matter of fact, the setting alone was genuine. Rétaux de Villette had preserved it, while Sieur de La Motte and his wife dispersed to the four winds of heaven the stones so brutally unmounted, the admirable stones once so carefully chosen by Böhmer. Later, Rétaux sold it, in Italy, to Gaston de Dreux-Sobise, the cardinal's nephew and heir, who had been saved by his uncle at the time of the notorious bankruptcy of the Rohan-Guéménée family, and who, in grateful memory of his kindness, bought up the few diamonds that remained in the possession of Jeffreys, the English jewel, completed them with others of smaller value, but of identical dimensions, and thus succeeded in reconstructing the wonderful necklace in the form in which it had left Böhmer and Bassagne's hands.

The Dreux-Soubises had prided themselves upon the possession of this ornament for nearly a century. Although their fortune had been considerably diminished by various circumstances, they preferred to reduce their establishment rather than part with the precious royal relic. The reigning count in particular clung to it as a man clings to the home of his fathers. For prudence' sake, he hired a safe at the Crédit Lyonnais in which to keep it. He always fetched it there himself on the afternoon of any day on which his wife proposed to wear it; and he as regularly took it back the next morning.

That evening, at the Palais de Castille, then occupied by Isabella II of Spain, the Countess had a great success, and King Christian of Denmark, in whose honour the reception was given, remarked upon her magnificent beauty. The gems streamed down her slender neck. The thousand facets of the diamonds shone and sparkled like flames in the light of the brilliantly illuminated rooms. None but she could have carried with such ease and dignity the burden of that marvellous jewel.

It was a twofold triumph which the Comte de Dreux enjoyed most thoroughly, and upon which he congratulated himself when they returned to their bedroom in the old house in the Faubourg Saint-Germain. He was proud of his wife, and quite as proud, perhaps, of the ornament which had shed its lustre upon his family for four generations. And the countess, too, derived from it a vanity which was a little childish, and yet quite in keeping with her haughty nature.

She took the necklace from her shoulders, not without regret, and handed it to her husband, who examined it with admiring eyes, as though he had never seen it before. Then, after replacing it in its red morocco case, stamped with the cardinal's arms, he went into an adjoining linen-closet, originally a sort of alcove, which had been cut off from the room, and which had only one entrance — a door at the foot of the bed. He hid it, according to his custom, among the band-boxes and stacks of linen on one of the upper shelves. He returned, closed the door behind him, and undressed himself.

In the morning he rose at nine o'clock, with the intention of going to the Crédit Lyonnais before lunch. He dressed, drank his coffee, and went down to the stables, where he gave his orders for the day. One of the horses seemed out of condition. He made the groom walk and trot it up and down before him in the yard. Then he went back to his wife.

She had not left the room, and was having her hair dressed by her maid. She said:

'Are you going out?'

'Yes, to take it back . . . '

'Oh, of course, yes, that will be safest . . . '

He entered the linen-closet. But in a few seconds he asked, without, however, displaying the least astonishment:

'Have you taken it out, dear?'

She replied:

'What do you mean? No, I've taken nothing.'

'But you moved it?'

'Not at all . . . I haven't even opened the door.'

He appeared in the doorway with a bewildered air, and stammered, in hardly intelligible accents:

'You haven't . . . you didn't . . . but then . . . '

She ran to join him, and they made a

feverish search, throwing the bandboxes to the floor, and demolishing the stacks of linen. And the count kept on saying:

'It's useless . . . All that we are doing is quite useless . . . I put it up here on this shelf.'

'You may have forgotten.'

'No, no; it was here, on this shelf, and nowhere else.'

They lit a candle, for the light in the little room was bad, and removed all the linen and all the different things with which it was crowded. And when the closet was quite empty they were compelled to admit, in despair, that the famous necklace, the Queen's Necklace, was gone.

The countess, who was noted for her determined character, wasted no time in vain lamentations, but sent for the commissary of police, M. Valorbe, whose sagacity and insight they had already had occasion to appreciate. He was put in possession of the details, and his first question was:

'Are you sure, monsieur le comte, that no one can have passed through your room at night?'

'Quite sure. I am a very light sleeper, and, besides, the bedroom door was bolted. I had to unfasten it this morning when my wife rang for the maid.'

'Is there no other inlet through which it is possible to enter the closet?'

'None.'

'No window?'

'Yes, but it is blocked up.'

'I should like to see it.'

Candles were lit, and M. Valorbe at once remarked that the window was only blocked halfway by a chest, which, besides, did not absolutely touch the casements.

'It is close enough up to prevent its being moved without making a great deal of noise.'

'What does the window look out on?'

'On a small inner yard.'

'And you have another floor above this?'

'Two; but at the level of the servants' floor the yard is protected by a close-railed grating. That is what makes the light so bad.'

Moreover, when they moved the chest they found that the window was latched, which would have been impossible if any one had entered from the outside.

'Unless,' said the count, 'he went out through our room.'

'In which case you would not have found the door bolted in the morning.'

The commissary reflected for a moment, and then, turning to the countess, asked:

'Did your people know, madame, that you were going to wear the necklace last night?'

'Certainly; I made no mystery about it. But nobody knew that we put it away in the linen-closet.'

'Nobody?'

'No . . . unless . . . '

'I must beg you, Madame, to be exact. It is a most important point.'

She said to her husband:

'I was thinking of Henriette.'

'Henriette? She knew no more about it than the others.'

'Who is this lady?' asked M. Valorbe.

'One of my convent friends who quarrelled with her family, and married a sort of artisan. When her husband died I took her in here with her son, and furnished a couple of rooms for them in the house.' And she added, with a certain confusion: 'She does me a few little services. She is a very handy person.'

'What floor does she live on?'

'On our own floor, not far off . . . at the end of the passage . . . And, now that I think of it, her kitchen window . . . '

'Looks out on this yard?'

'Yes, it is just opposite.'

A short silence followed upon this statement.

Then M. Valorbe asked to be taken to Henriette's rooms.

They found her busy sewing, while her son

Raoul, a little fellow of six or seven, sat reading beside her. Somewhat surprised at the sight of the poor apartment which had been furnished for her, and which consisted in all of one room without a fireplace, and of a sort of recess or box-room that did duty for a kitchen, the commissary questioned her. She seemed upset at hearing of the robbery. The night before she had herself dressed the countess, and fastened the necklace round her throat.

'Good gracious!' she exclaimed, 'who would have ever thought it?'

'And you have no idea, not the smallest inkling? You know it is possible that the thief may have passed through your room.'

She laughed whole-heartedly, as though not imagining for a moment that the least suspicion could rest upon her.

'Why, I never left my room! I never go out, you know. And, besides, look!' She opened the window of the kitchen. 'There, it's quite three yards to the ledge opposite.'

'Who told you that we were considering the likelihood of a theft committed by this way?'

'Why, wasn't the necklace in the closet?'

'How do you know?'

'Goodness me, I always knew that they put it there at night! . . . They used to talk of it before me . . . '

Her face, which was still young, but scored by care and sorrow, showed great gentleness and resignation. Nevertheless, in the silence that ensued, it suddenly assumed an expression of anguish, as though a danger had threatened its owner. Henriette drew her son to her. The child took her hand, and impressed a tender kiss upon it.

'I presume,' said M. de Dreux to the commissary, when they were alone again, 'I presume that you do not suspect her? I will answer for her. She is honesty itself.'

'Oh, I am quite of your opinion,' declared M. Valorbe. 'At most, the thought of an unconscious complicity passed through my mind. But I can see that we must abandon this explanation . . . it does not in the least help to solve the problem that faces us.'

The commissary did not arrive any further with the inquiry, which was taken up by the examining magistrate, and completed in the course of the days that followed. He questioned the servants, experimented on the way in which the window of the linen-closet opened and shut, explored the little inner yard from top to bottom . . . It was all fruitless. The latch was untouched. The window could not be opened or closed from the outside.

The inquiries were aimed more particularly

at Henriette, for, in spite of everything, the question always reverted in her direction. Her life was carefully investigated. It was ascertained that in three years she had only four times left the house, and it was possible to trace her movements on each of these occasions. As a matter of fact, she served Madame de Dreux in the capacity of lady's maid and dressmaker, and her mistress treated her with a strictness to which all the servants, in confidence, bore witness.

'Besides,' said the magistrate, who, by the end of the first week, had come to the same conclusions as the commissary, 'admitting that we know the culprit — and we do not — we are no wiser as to the manner in which the theft was committed. We are hemmed in on either side by two obstacles — a locked window and a locked door. There are two mysteries: How could the thief get in? and, more difficult still, how could he get out, and leave a bolted door and a latched window behind him?'

After four months' investigation the magistrate's private impression was that M. and Mme. de Dreux, driven by their monetary needs, which were known to be considerable and pressing, had sold the Queen's Necklace. He filed the case, and dismissed it from his mind.

The theft of the priceless jewel struck the Dreux-Soubises a blow from which it took them long to recover. Now that their credit was no longer sustained by the sort of reserve-fund which the possession of that treasure constituted, they found themselves confronted with less reasonable creditors and less willing money-lenders. They were compelled to resort to energetic measures, to sell and mortgage their property; in short, it would have meant absolute ruin if two fat legacies from distant relatives had not come in the nick of time to save them.

They also suffered in their pride, as though they had lost one of the quarterings of their coat. And, strange to say, the countess wreaked her resentment upon her old school friend. She bore a real grudge, and accused her openly. Henriette was first banished to the servants' floor, and afterwards given a day's notice to quit.

The life of M. and Mme. de Dreux passed without any event of note. They travelled a great deal.

One fact alone must be recorded as belonging to this period. A few months after Henriette's departure the countess received a letter from her that filled her with amazement:

'Madame–I do not know how to thank you. For it was you, was it not, who sent me that? It must have been you. No one else knows of my retreat in this little village. Forgive me if I am mistaken, and, in any case, accept the expression of my gratitude for your past kindnesses.'

What did she mean? The countess' past and present kindnesses to Henriette amounted to a number of acts of injustice. What was the meaning of these thanks?

Henriette was called upon to explain, and replied that she had received by post, in an unregistered envelope, two notes of a thousand francs each. She enclosed the envelope in her letter. It was stamped with the Paris post-mark, and bore only her address, written in an obviously disguised hand.

Where did that two thousand francs come from? Who had sent it? And why had it been sent? The police made inquiries. But what possible clue could they follow up in that darkness?

The same incident was repeated twelve months later; and a third time; and a fourth time; and every year for six years, with this difference: that in the fifth and sixth year the amount sent was doubled, which enabled Henriette, who had suddenly fallen ill, to provide for proper nursing. There was another difference: the postal authorities having seized one of the letters, on the pretext that it was not registered, the two last letters were handed in for registration — one at Saint-Germain, the other at Suresnes. The sender had signed his name first as Anquerty, next as Péchard. The addresses which he gave were false.

At the end of six years Henriette died. The riddle remained unsolved.

★ ★ ★

All these particulars are matters of public knowledge. The case was one of those which stir men's minds, and it was strange that this necklace, after setting all France by the ears at the end of the eighteenth century, should succeed in causing so much renewed excitement more than a hundred years later. But what I am now about to relate is known to none, except the principals interested and a few persons upon whom the count imposed absolute secrecy. As it is probable that they will break their promises sooner or later, I have no scruple in tearing aside the veil; and thus my readers will receive, together with the key to the riddle, the explanation of the paragraph that appeared in the newspapers two mornings ago — an extraordinary paragraph, which added, if possible, a fresh modicum of darkness and mystery to the obscurity in which this drama was already shrouded.

We must go five days back. Among M. de Dreux-Soubise's guests at lunch were his two nieces and a cousin; the men were the Président d'Essaville; M. Bachas, the deputy; The Chevalier Floriani, whom the count had met in Sicily; and General the Marquis de Rouzières, an old club acquaintance.

After lunch, the ladies served coffee in the drawing room, and the gentlemen were given leave to smoke, on condition that they stayed where they were and talked. One of the girls amused them by telling their fortunes on the cards. The conversation afterwards turned on the subject of celebrated crimes. And thereupon M. de Rouzières, who never neglected an opportunity of teasing the count, brought up the affair of the necklace — a subject which M. de Dreux detested.

Everyone proceeded to give his opinion. Everyone summed up the evidence in his own way. And, of course, all the conclusions were contradictory, and all equally inadmissible.

'And what is your opinion, monsieur?'

asked the countess of the Chevalier Floriani.

'Oh, I have no opinion, Madame'

There was a general outcry of protest, inasmuch as the chevalier had only just been most brilliantly describing a series of adventures in which he had taken part with his father, a magistrate at Palermo, and in which he had given evidence of his taste for these matters and of his sound judgment.

'I confess,' he said, 'that I have sometimes managed to succeed where the experts had abandoned all their attempts. But I am far from considering myself a Sherlock Holmes . . . And, besides, I hardly know the facts . . .'

All faces were turned to the master of the house, who was reluctantly compelled to recapitulate the details. The chevalier listened, reflected, put a few questions, and murmured:

'It's odd . . . at first sight the thing does not seem to me so difficult to guess at.'

The count shrugged his shoulders. But the others flocked round the chevalier, who resumed, in a rather dogmatic tone:

'As a general rule, in order to discover the author of a theft or other crime, we have first to determine how this theft or crime has been committed, or at least how it might have been committed. In the present case nothing could be simpler, in my view, for we find ourselves face to face not with a number of different suppositions, but with one hard certainty, which is that the individual was able to enter only by the door of the bedroom or the window of the linen-closet. Now, a bolted door cannot be opened from the outside. Therefore, he must have entered by the window.'

'It was closed, and it was found closed,' said M. de Dreux, flatly.

Floriani took no notice of the interruption, and continued:

'In order to do so he had only to fix a bridge of some sort — say, a plank or a ladder — between the balcony outside the kitchen and the ledge of the window; and, as soon as the jewel-case . . . '

'But I tell you the window was closed!' cried the count, impatiently.

This time Floriani was obliged to reply. He did so with the greatest calmness, like a man who refuses to be put out by so insignificant an objection.

'I have no doubt that it was. But was there no hinged pane or transom?'

'What makes you think so?'

'To begin with, it is almost a rule in the casement windows of that period. And, next, there must have been one, because otherwise the theft would be inexplicable.'

'As a matter of fact, there was one, but it was closed, like the window. We did not even pay attention to it.'

'That was a mistake; for if you had paid attention to it, you would obviously have seen that it had been opened.'

'And how?'

'I presume that, like all of them, it opens by means of a twisted iron wire, furnished with a ring at its lower end?'

'Yes.'

'And did this ring hand down between the casement and the chest?'

'Yes, but I do not understand . . . '

'It is like this. Through some cleft or cranny in the pane they must have contrived, with the aid of an instrument of some sort — say, an iron rod ending in a hook — to grip the ring, press down upon it, and open the pane.'

The count sneered.

'That's perfect! Perfect! You settle it all so easily! Only you have forgotten one thing, my dear sir, which is that there was no cleft or cranny in the pane.'

'Oh, but there was!'

'How can you say that? We should have seen it.'

'To see a thing one must look, and you did not look. The cleft exists, it is materially impossible that it should not exist, down the side of the pane, along the putty . . . vertically, of course . . . '

The count rose. He seemed greatly excited, took two or three nervous strides across the room, and, going up to Floriani, said:

'Nothing has been changed up there since that day . . . no one has set foot in that closet.'

'In that case, monsieur, it is open to you to assure yourself that my explanation is in accordance with reality.'

'It is in accordance with none of the facts which the police ascertained. You have seen nothing, you know nothing, and you go counter to all that we have seen and to all that we know.'

Floriani did not seem to remark the count's irritation, and said, with a smile:

'Well, monsieur, I am trying to see plainly, that is all. If I am wrong you have only to prove me so . . . '

'So I will, this very minute . . . I confess that, in the long run, your assurance . . . '

M. de Dreux mumbled a few words more, and then suddenly turned to the door and went out.

No one spoke a word. All waited anxiously, as though convinced that a particle of the truth was about to appear. And the silence was marked by an extreme gravity.

At last the count was seen standing in the doorway. He was pale, and singularly agitated. He addressed his friends in a voice trembling with emotion:

'I beg your pardon . . . Monsieur Floriani's revelations have taken me so greatly by surprise . . . I should never have thought . . . '

His wife asked him eagerly:

'What is it? . . . Tell us! . . . Speak! . . . '

He stammered out:

'The cleft is there . . . at the very place mentioned . . . down the side of the pane . . . '

Abruptly seizing the chevalier's arm, he said, in an imperious tone:

'And now, monsieur, continue . . . I admit that you have been right so far, but now . . . That is not all . . . Tell me . . . what happened, according to you?'

Floriani gently released his arm, and, after a moment's interval, said:

'Well, according to me, this is what happened: The individual, whoever he was, knowing that Madame de Dreux was going to wear the necklace at the reception, put his foot-bridge in position during your absence. He watched you through the window, and saw you hide the diamonds. As soon as you were gone he passed some implement down the pane and pulled the ring.'

'Very well; but the distance was too great to allow of his reaching the latch of the window through the transom.'

'If he was unable to open the window he must have got in through the transom itself.'

'Impossible; there is not a man so slight in figure as to obtain admission that way.'

'Then it was not a man.'

'What do you mean?'

'What I say. If the passage was too narrow to admit a man, then it must have been a child.'

'A child?'

'Did you not tell me that your friend had a son?'

'I did; a son named Raoul.'

'It is extremely likely that Raoul committed the theft.'

'What evidence have you?'

'What evidence? . . . There is no lack of evidence . . . For instance . . . ' He was silent, and reflected for a few seconds. Then he continued: 'For instance, it is incredible that the child could have brought a footbridge from outside and taken it away again unperceived. He must have employed what lay ready to hand. In the little room where Henriette did her cooking, were there not some shelves against the wall on which she kept her pots and pans?'

'There were two shelves, as far as I remember.'

'We must find out if these shelves were really fixed to the wooden brackets that support them. If so, we are entitled to believe that the child unscrewed them and then fastened them together. Perhaps, also, if there was a range, we shall discover a stove-hook or plate-lifter which he would have employed to open the hinged pane.'

The count went out without a word, and this time the others did not even feel that little touch of anxiety attendant upon the unknown which they had experienced on the first occasion. They knew, they knew absolutely, that Floriani's view were correct. There emanated from that man an impression of such strict certainty that they listened to him not as though he were deducting facts one from the other, but as though he were describing events the accuracy of which it was easy to verify as he proceeded. And no one felt surprised when the count returned and said:

'Yes, it's the child . . . there's no doubt about it . . . everything proves it . . . '

'Did you see the shelves . . . the plate-lifter?'

But Madame de Dreux-Soubise exclaimed: 'The child! . . . You mean his mother.

Henriette is the only guilty person. She must have compelled her son to . . . '

'No,' said the chevalier, 'the mother had nothing to do with it.'

'Come, come! They lived in the same room; the child cannot have acted unknown to Henriette.'

'They occupied the same room; but everything happened in the adjoining recess, at night, while the mother was asleep.'

'And what about the necklace?' said the count. 'It would have been found among the child's things.'

'I beg your pardon. 'He' used to go out. The very morning when you found him with his book he had come back from school, and perhaps the police, instead of exhausting their resources against the innocent mother, would have been better advised to make a search there, in his desk, among his lesson-books.'

'Very well. But the two thousand francs which Henriette received every year: is not that the best sign of her complicity?'

'Would she have written to thank you for the money if she had been an accomplice? Besides, was she not kept under supervision? Whereas the child was free, and had every facility for going to the nearest town, seeing a dealer, and selling him a diamond cheaply, or two diamonds, as the case demanded . . . the only condition being that the money should be sent from Paris, in consideration of which the transaction would be repeated next year.'

The Dreux-Soubises and their guests were oppressed by an undefinable sense of uneasiness. There was really in Floriani's tone and attitude something more than that certainty which had so irritated the count from the beginning. There was something resembling irony — an irony, moreover, that seemed hostile rather than sympathetic and friendly, as it ought to have been. The count affected a laugh.

'All of this is delightfully ingenious. Accept my compliments. What a brilliant imagination you possess!'

'No, no, no!' cried Floriani, with more seriousness. 'I am not imagining anything; I am recalling circumstances which were inevitably such as I have described them to you.'

'What do you know of them?'

'What you yourself have told me. I picture the life of the mother and the child down there in the country: the mother falling ill, the tricks and inventions of the little fellow to sell the stones and save his mother, or at least to ease her last moments. Her illness carries her off. She dies. Years pass. The child grows up, becomes a man. And then — this time, I am willing to admit that I am giving scope to my imagination — suppose that this man should feel a longing to return to the places where his childhood was spent, that he sees them once again, that he finds the people who have suspected and accused his mother: think of the poignant interest of such an interview in the old house under whose roof the different stages of the drama were enacted!'

His words echoed for a moment or two in the restless silence, and the faces of M. and Mme. de Dreux revealed a desperate endeavour to understand, combined with an agonizing dread of understanding. The count asked, between his teeth:

'Tell me, sir! Who are you?'

'I? Why, the Chevalier Floriani, whom you met at Palermo, and whom you have had the kindness to invite to your house time after time.'

'Then what is the meaning of this story?'

'Oh, nothing at all! It is a mere joke on my part. I am trying to picture to myself the delight which Henriette's son, if he were still alive, would take in telling you that he is the only culprit, and that he became so because his mother was on the point of losing her place as a . . . as a domestic servant, which was her only means of livelihood, and because the child suffered at the sight of his mother's unhappiness.'

He had half risen from his seat, and, bending towards the countess, was expressing himself in terms of suppressed emotion. There was no doubt possible. The Chevalier Floriani was none other than Henriette's son. Everything in his attitude, in his words, proclaimed the fact. Besides, was it not his evident intention, his wish, to be recognized as such?

The count hesitated. What line of conduct was he to adopt towards this daring individual? To ring the bell? Provoke a scandal? Unmask the villain who had robbed him? But it was so long ago! And who would believe this story of a guilty child? No, it was better to accept the position and pretend not to grasp its real meaning. And the count, going up to Floriani, said, playfully:

'Your little romance is very interesting and very entertaining. It has quite taken hold of me, I assure you. But, according to you, what became of that exemplary young man, this model son? I trust he did not stop on his prosperous road to fortune.'

'Certainly not!'

'Why, of course not! After so fine a start, too! At the age of six to capture the Queen's Necklace, the celebrated necklace coveted by Marie-Antoinette!'

'And to capture it, mind you,' said Floriani, entering into the count's mood, 'to capture it without its costing him the smallest unpleasantness, the police never taking it into their heads to examine the condition of the panes, or noticing that the window-ledge was too clean after he had wiped it so as to obliterate the traces of his feet on the thick dust . . . You must admit that this was enough to turn the head of a scapegrace of his years. It was all too easy. He had only to wish and put out his hand . . . Well, he wished . . . '

'And put out his hand?'

'Both hands!' replied the chevalier, with a smile.

A shudder passed through his hearers. What mystery concealed the life of this self-styled Floriani? How extraordinary must be the existence of this adventurer, a gifted thief at the age of six, who today, with the refined taste of a dilettante in search of an emotion, or, at most, to satisfy a sense of revenge, had come to brave his victim in that victim's own house, audaciously, madly, and yet with all the good-breeding of a man of the world on a visit!

He rose, and went up to the countess to take his leave. She suppressed a movement of recoil. He smiled.

'Ah, Madame, you are frightened! Have I

carried my little comedy of parlour magician too far?'

'Not at all, monsieur. On the contrary, the legend of that good son has interested me greatly, and I am happy to think that my necklace should have been the occasion of so brilliant a career. But does it not seem to you that the son of that . . . of that woman, of Henriette, was, above all things, obeying his natural upbringing?'

He started, felt the point of her remark, and replied:

'I am sure he was; and, in fact, his upbringing must have been quite strong, or the child would have been discouraged.'

'Why?'

'Well, you know, most of the stones were false. The only real ones were the few diamonds bought of the English jeweller. The others had been sold, one by one, in obedience to the stern necessities of life.'

'It was the Queen's Necklace, monsieur, for all that,' said the countess, haughtily, 'and that, it seems to me, is what Henriette's son was unable to understand.'

'He must have understood, Madame, that, false or genuine, the necklace was, before all, a show thing, a sign-board.'

M. de Dreux made a movement. His wife stopped him at once.

'Monsieur,' she said, 'if the man to whom you allude has the least sense of honour . . .'

She hesitated, shrinking before Floriani's calm gaze. He repeated after her:

'If he has the least feeling of honour . . .'

She felt that she would gain nothing by speaking to him in this way; and, despite her anger and indignation, quivering with humiliated pride, she said, almost politely:

'Monsieur, tradition says that Rétaux de Villette, when the Queen's Necklace was in his hands, forced out all the diamonds with Jeanne de Valois, but he dared not touch the setting. He understood that the diamonds were but the ornaments, the accessories, whereas the setting was the essential work, the creation of the artist; and he respected it. Do you think that this man understood as much?'

'I have no doubt but that the setting exists. The child respected it.'

'Well, monsieur, if ever you happen to meet him, tell him that he is acting unjustly in keeping one of those relics which are the property and glory of certain families, and that though he may have removed the stones, the Queen's Necklace continues to belong to the house of Dreux-Soubise. It is ours as much as our name or our honour.'

The chevalier replied, simply:

'I will tell him so, Madame'

He bowed low before her, bowed to the count, bowed to all the visitors, one after the other, and went out.

★ ★ ★

Four days later Madame de Dreux found a red morocco case, stamped with the arms of the Cardinal de Rohan, on her bedroom table. She opened it. It contained the necklace of Marie-Antoinette.

But as in the life of any logical and single-minded man all things must needs concur towards the same object — and as a little advertisement never does any harm — the Echo de France of the next day contained the following sensational paragraph:

'The Queen's Necklace, the famous historic jewel stolen many years ago since from the Dreux-Soubise family, has been recovered by Arsène Lupin. Arsène Lupin has hastened to restore it to its lawful owners. This delicate and chivalrous act is sure to meet with universal commendation.'

The Seven of Hearts

I have often been asked this question:

'How did you come to know Arsène Lupin?'

No one doubts that I know him. The details which I am able to heap up concerning his bewildering personality, the undeniable facts which I set forth, the fresh proofs which I supply, the interpretation which I provide of certain acts of which others have seen only the outward manifestations, without following their secret reasons or their invisible mechanism: all this points, if not to an intimacy, which Lupin's very existence would render impossible, at least to friendly relations and an uninterrupted confidence.

But how did I come to know him? Why was I favoured to the extent of becoming his biographer? Why I rather than another?

The answer presents no difficulty: accident alone determined a selection in which my personal merit goes for nothing. It was accident that threw me across his path. It was by accident that I was mixed up in one of his most curious and mysterious adventures; by

153

accident, lastly, that I became an actor in a drama of which he was the wonderful stage-manager, an obscure and complicated drama bristling with such extraordinary catastrophes that I feel a certain perplexity as I sit down to describe them.

The first act passes in the course of that famous night of the twenty-second of June which has been so much discussed. And I may as well at once confess that I attribute my somewhat abnormal conduct on that occasion to the very peculiar condition of mind in which I found myself when I returned home. I had been dining with friends at the Restaurant de la Cascade, and throughout the evening, while we sat smoking and listening to the Bohemian band and their melancholy waltzes, we had talked of nothing but crimes, robberies, lurid and terrifying adventures. This is always a bad preparation for sleep.

The Saint-Martins had driven away in their motor-car. Jean Daspry — the charming, reckless Daspry, who was to meet his death, six months later, in so tragic a fashion, on the Morocco frontier — Jean Daspry and I walked back in the dark, hot night. When we reached the little house at Neuilly, on the Boulevard Maillot, where I had been living for the past twelve months, he said:

'Do you never feel frightened?'

'What an idea!'

'Well, this little house of yours is very lonely: no neighbours ... surrounded by waste land ... I'm no coward, as you know. And yet ... '

'By Jove, you're in a cheerful mood to-night!'

'Oh, I said that as I might have said anything else. The Saint-Martins have impressed me with their stories about burglars and highwaymen.'

We shook hands, and he walked away. I took out my key, and opened the door.

'That's pleasant!' I muttered. 'Antoine has forgotten to leave a lighted candle for me.'

And suddenly I remembered: Antoine was out; I had given him his night off.

I at once resented the darkness and the silence. I groped my way upstairs to my room as quickly as I could, and, contrary to my custom, turned the key in the door, and shot the bolt.

The light of the candle restored my presence of mind. Nevertheless, I was careful to take my revolver — a big, long-range revolver — from its case, and laid it beside my bed. This precaution completed my composure. I went to bed, and, as usual, took up the book that lay on my night-table to read myself to sleep.

A great surprise awaited me. In the place of the paper-cutter with which I had marked my page the night before I now found an envelope sealed with five red seals. I seized it eagerly. It was addressed in my name, accompanied by the word 'Urgent.'

A letter! A letter addressed to me! Who could have put it there? Somewhat nervously I tore open the envelope, and read:

'From the moment when you open this letter, whatever happens, whatever you may hear, do not stir, do not make a movement, do not utter a sound. If you do, you are lost.'

Now I am not a coward, and I know as well as another how a man should bear himself in the presence of real danger or smile at the fanciful perils that alarm our imagination. But, I repeat, I was in an abnormal and easily impressionable frame of mind; my nerves were on edge. Besides, was there not something perturbing in all this, something inexplicable — enough to trouble the most undaunted soul?

My fingers feverishly pressed the sheet of notepaper, and my eyes incessantly read and reread the threatening words:

'Do not make a movement, do not utter a sound. If you do, you are lost.'

'Nonsense!' I thought. 'It's a joke, a silly trick!'

I was on the point of laughing, I even tried to laugh aloud. What was it that prevented me? What vague fear compressed my throat?

At least, I would blow out the candle. No, I could not blow it out.

'Not a movement, or you are lost,' said the letter.

But why struggle against this kind of auto-suggestion, which is often more urgent than the most precise facts? There was nothing to do but to close my eyes. I closed my eyes.

At that moment a light sound passed through the silence, followed by a creaking noise. It seemed to me to come from a large adjoining room which I had fitted up as a study, and from which I was separated only by the passage.

The approach of real danger excited me, and I felt that I was going to jump up, seize my revolver, and rush into the other room. I did not jump up. One of the curtains of the window on my left had moved before my eyes.

There was no doubt possible; it had moved. It was still moving! And I saw — oh, I distinctly saw! — that in that narrow space between the curtains and the window there stood a human form, the thickness of which prevented the material from hanging down straight.

And the being saw me, too; it was certain that he could see me through the wide meshes of the stuff. Then I understood all. While the others were carrying off their booty, his mission consisted in terrorizing me. Jump out of bed? Seize a revolver? It was impossible . . . he was there! At the least movement, at the least sound, I was lost.

A violent blow shook the house, followed by smaller blows, in twos and threes, like those of a hammer driving in tacks and rebounding — or, at least, that was what I imagined in the confusion of my brain; and other noises followed, a regular din of different noises, which proved that my visitors were doing as they pleased and acting in all security.

They were right: I did not budge. Was it cowardice on my part? No, it was annihilation rather, a complete incapacity to move a single muscle. Prudence also; for, after all, why struggle? Behind that man were ten others, who would come at his call. Was it worth while to risk my life to save a few hangings and knick-knacks?

And this torture lasted all night long: an intolerable torture, a terrible agony! The noise had stopped, but I never ceased waiting for it to begin again! And the man, the man who stood there watching me, weapon in hand! My terrified gaze never left him. And my heart beat, and the perspiration streamed from my forehead and my whole body!

Suddenly I was pervaded by an unspeakable sense of relief: a milk-cart, of which I knew the clatter well, passed along the boulevard; and at the same time, I received the impression that the dawn was filtering through the drawn blinds, and that a glimmer of daylight from the outside was mingling with the darkness within.

And the light entered my room. And other vehicles passed. And all the phantoms of the night vanished.

Then I put one arm out of bed slowly and stealthily. Opposite me nothing stirred. With my eyes I noted the fold in the curtain, the exact spot at which to take aim. I made a precise calculation of the movements which I should have to make. I grasped the revolver — and I fired.

I sprang out of bed with a shout of deliverance, and leaped at the curtain. There was a hole through the material, and a hole in the pane behind it. As for the man, I had missed him . . . for the very good reason that there was nobody there.

Nobody! And so all night long I had been hypnotized by a fold in a curtain! And during that time, criminals had . . . Furiously, with an impulse which nothing could have stopped, I turned the key in the lock, opened my door, crossed the passage, opened another door, and rushed into the room.

But a feeling of stupefaction rooted me to the threshold, panting, dumfounded, even more astonished than I had been by the absence of the man: nothing had disappeared! All the things which I had expected to find gone — furniture, pictures, old silks, and velvets — all these things were in their places!

It was an incomprehensible sight. I could not believe my eyes. And yet that din, those noises of moving furniture . . . I went all round the room, inspected the walls, took an inventory of all the objects which I knew so well. There was not a thing missing! And what disconcerted me most of all was that nothing either revealed the passing of the evil-doers — not a sign, not a chair out of place, not a footmark.

'Come, come,' I said, clasping my head with my two hands, 'after all, I'm not a madman! I heard what I heard! . . . '

I examined the room inch by inch, employing the most minute methods of investigation; it was to no purpose. Or, rather

... but could I consider that a discovery? Under a small Persian rug, flung down on the floor, I picked up a card — a playing-card. It was a seven of hearts, similar to the seven of hearts in any French pack of cards; but it attracted my attention because of a rather curious detail. The extreme lower end of each of the seven red, heart-shaped pips was pierced with a hole, the round and regular hole made by the point of an awl.

That, and no more. A card, and a letter found in a book! Beyond that, nothing. Was this enough to avouch that I had not been the sport of a dream?

I pursued my investigations throughout the day. It was a large-sized room, out of all proportion with the general smallness of the house, and its decoration bore witness to the eccentric taste of the man who had conceived it. The floor was made of a mosaic of tiny, parti-coloured stones, forming large symmetrical designs. The walls were covered with a similar mosaic, arranged in panels representing Pompeiian allegories, Byzantine compositions, mediaeval frescoes: a Bacchus sat astride a barrel; an emperor with a golden crown and a flowing beard held a sword uplifted in his right hand.

High up in the wall was a huge solitary window, something like the window of a studio. It was always left open at night, and the probability was that the men had entered by it with the aid of a ladder. But here again there was no certainty. The posts of the ladder would necessarily have left marks on the trodden ground of the yard: there were no such marks. The grass of the waste land surrounding the house would have been freshly trampled: it was not.

I confess that the idea of applying to the police never entered my head, so inconsistent and absurd were the facts which I should have had to lay before them. They would have laughed at me. But the next day but one was the day for my column in the Gil Blas, for which I was then writing. Obsessed as I was by my adventure, I described it at full length.

My article attracted some little attention, but I could see that it was not taken seriously, and that it was looked upon as a fanciful rather than a true story. The Saint-Martins chaffed me about it. Daspry, however, who was something of an expert in these matters, came to see me, made me explain the whole case to him, and studied it . . . but with no more success than myself.

A few mornings later the bell at the front gate rang, and Antoine came to tell me that a gentleman wished to speak to me. He had refused to give his name. I asked him up.

He was a man of about forty, with a very dark complexion and strongly marked features; and his clothes, which, though greatly worn, were neat and clean, proclaimed a taste for fashion that contrasted with his manners, which were rather common.

Coming straight to the point, he said, in a grating voice, and in an accent that confirmed my opinion as to the man's social status:

'I have been out of town, sir, and I saw the Gil Blas at a cafe. I read your article. It interested me . . . immensely.'

'I thank you.'

'And I came back.'

'Ah!'

'Yes, to see you. Are all the facts which you describe correct?'

'Absolutely correct.'

'Is there not a single one invented by yourself?'

'Not a single one.'

'In that case, I may have some information to give you.'

'Pray speak.'

'No.'

'How do you mean?'

'Before saying any more, I must make sure that I am right.'

'And to do that? . . . '

'I must remain alone in this room.'

I looked at him in surprise.

'I don't quite see . . . '

'It's an idea that came to me on reading your article. Certain details establish a really remarkable coincidence between your adventure and another which was revealed to me by chance. If I am wrong, it would be better for me to keep silence. And the only way of finding out is for me to remain alone . . . '

What was there underlying this proposal? Later I remembered that, in making it, the man wore an uneasy air, an anxious look. But at the same time, although feeling a little astonished, I saw nothing particularly abnormal in his request. And, besides, his curiosity stimulated me.

I replied:

'Very well. How long do you want?'

'Oh, three minutes, that's all. I shall join you in three minutes from now.'

I left the room and went downstairs. I took out my watch. One minute passed. Two minutes . . . What gave me that sense of oppression? Why did those moments seem to me more solemn than any others? . . .

Two minutes and a half . . . Two minutes and three-quarters . . . And suddenly a shot resounded.

I rushed up the stairs in half a dozen

strides, and entered the room. A cry of horror escaped me.

The man lay motionless, on his left side, in the middle of the floor. Blood trickled from his head, mingled with portions of brains. A smoking revolver lay close by his hand.

He gave a single convulsion, and that was all.

But there was something that struck me even more than this awful sight — something that was the reason why I did not at once call out for help, nor fling myself on my knees to see if the man was still breathing: at two paces from him a seven of hearts lay on the floor!

I picked it up. The lower point of each of the seven pips was pierced with a hole . . .

*   *   *

Half an hour later the commissary of police of Neuilly arrived, followed, in a few moments, by the police surgeon, and by M. Dudouis, the head of the detective service. I was careful not the touch the corpse. There was nothing to interfere with their first observations.

These were brief, the more so as, at the beginning, the officers discovered nothing, or very little. There were no papers in the dead man's pockets, no name on his clothes, no initials on his linen; in short, there was no clew whatever to his identity.

And in the room itself the same order prevailed as before. The furniture had not been moved, the different objects were all in their old places. And yet the man had not come to see me with the sole intention of killing himself, or because he considered my house better suited than another for the purpose of committing suicide. There must have been some motive to drive him to this act of despair, and this motive must have resulted from some new fact ascertained by himself in the course of the three minutes which he had spent alone.

But what fact? What had he seen? What had he discovered? What frightful secret had he surprised?

At the last moment, however, an incident occurred which seemed to us of great importance. Two policemen were stooping to lift the corpse in order to carry it away on a stretcher when they perceived that the left hand, till then closed and shrunk, had become relaxed, and a crumpled visiting-card fell from it. The card bore the words:

Georges Andermatt
37, Rue de Berry

What did this mean? Georges Andermatt was a big Paris banker, the founder and chairman of the Metal Exchange, which has done so much to forward the prospects of the metal trade in France. He lived in great style, kept a drag, motor-cars, a racing-stable. His parties were very much frequented, and Madame Andermatt was well known for her charm and her personal beauty.

'Could that be the man's name?' I murmured.

The head of the detective service bent over the corpse.

'No. Monsieur Andermatt is a pale-faced man, with hair just turning grey.'

'But why that card?'

'Have you a telephone, sir?'

'Yes, it's in the hall. If you will come this way . . . '

He turned up the directory, and asked for number 415.21.

'Is Monsieur Andermatt in? . . . My name is Dudouis . . . Please ask him to come with all speed to 102, Boulevard Maillot. It's urgent.'

Twenty minutes later M. Andermatt stepped out of his car. He was told the reason why he had been sent for, and was then taken upstairs to see the body.

He had a momentary emotion that

contracted his features, and said, in an undertone, as though involuntarily:

'Etienne Varin.'

'Do you know him?'

'No . . . or, at least, yes . . . but only by sight. His brother . . . '

'He has a brother?'

'Yes, Alfred Varin . . . His brother used to come and ask me to assist him . . . I have forgotten in what connection . . . '

'Where does he live?'

'The two brothers used to live together . . . in the Rue de Provence, I think.'

'And have you no suspicion of the reason why he shot himself?'

'None at all.'

'Still, he was holding your card in his hand . . . your card, with your name and address.'

'I can't understand it. It's obviously a mere accident which the inquiry will explain.'

It was, in any case, a very curious accident, I thought, and I felt that we all received the same impression.

I noticed this impression again in the papers of the next morning, and among all my friends with whom I discussed the circumstances. Amid the mysteries that complicated it, after the renewed and disconcerting discovery of that seven of hearts seven times pierced — after the two incidents, each as puzzling as the other, of which my house had been the scene — that visiting-card seemed at last to promise a glimpse of light. By its means they would arrive at the truth.

But, contrary to the general expectation, M. Andermatt furnished not a single clew.

'I have said all that I know,' he repeated. 'What can I do more? I was the first to be thunderstruck by the fact that my card was found where it was; and, like everybody else, I shall expect this point to be cleared up.'

It was not cleared up. The inquiry established that the Varins were two brothers, of Swiss origin, who had led a very chequered life under different aliases, frequenting the gambling-houses and connected with a whole gang of foreigners whose movements had been watched, and who had dispersed after a series of burglaries in which their participation was not proved until later. At No. 24, Rue de Provence, where the brothers Varin had, in fact, lived six years before, no one knew what had become of them.

I confess that, for my part, the case seemed to me so intricate that I scarcely believed in the possibility of a solution, and I tried hard to banish it from my mind. But Jean Daspry, on the contrary — and I saw a great deal of him at that time — grew daily more enthusiastic about it. It was he that called my attention to the following paragraph from a foreign paper, which was reproduced and commented upon throughout the press of the country:

'A new submarine is to be tried shortly in the presence of the Emperor. It is claimed on behalf of this vessel that her class will revolutionize the conditions of naval warfare in the future. The place of the trial will be kept secret until the last moment; but the name of the submarine has leaked out, through an indiscretion in official circles: she is called the Seven of Hearts.'

The Seven of Hearts! Was this a chance coincidence? Or did it establish a link between the name of the new submarine and the incidents of which we have spoken? But what sort of link? Surely, there could be no possible connection between what was happening here and in Germany?

'How do you know?' said Daspry. 'The most incongruous effects often arise from one and the same cause.'

Two days later another piece of news was reprinted from the German papers:

'It is now contended that the Seven of Hearts, the submarine whose trials are to take place forthwith, has been designed by French engineers. These engineers, after vainly seeking the support of their own government, are said to have applied next, and with no more success, to the British Admiralty. We need hardly say that we publish this statement with all reserve.'

I do not wish to insist too much upon the facts of an extremely delicate character which provoked considerable excitement, as the reader will remember, in France. Nevertheless, since all danger of international complications is now removed, I must speak of an article in the Echo de France which made a great deal of noise at the time, and which threw a more or less vague light upon 'The Seven of Hearts Affair,' as it was called.

Here it is, as it appeared under the signature of 'Salvator':

THE SEVEN OF HEARTS AFFAIR: A CORNER OF THE VEIL RAISED

We will be brief. Ten years ago Louis Lacombe, a young engineer in the mines, wishing to devote his time and money to the studies which he was pursuing, resigned his appointment, and hired a small house, at 102, Boulevard Maillot, which had recently been built and decorated by an Italian nobleman.

Through the intermediary of two brothers called Varin, of Lausanne, one of whom assisted him as a preparator of his experiments, while the other went in search of financial bankers for his schemes, Lacombe entered into relations with M. Georges Andermatt, who had then just founded the Paris Metal Exchange.

After a number of interviews he succeeded in interesting M. Andermatt in the plans of a submarine upon which he was engaged; and it was understood that, as soon as the invention had been definitely perfected, M. Andermatt would employ his influence to persuade the Minister of Marine to grant a series of trials.

For two years Louis Lacombe was constantly visiting the Hotel Andermatt, and submitting his improvements to the banker, until the day came when, having lighted upon the final formula which he was seeking and being fully satisfied with his labours, he asked M. Andermatt to set to work on his side.

On that day Louis Lacombe dined at the Andermatts'. He left the house at half-past eleven in the evening. Since *then he has not been seen by mortal eyes.*

On reading the newspapers of the day we find that the young man's family called in the police, and that the public prosecutor took the matter up. But the inquiries led to nothing, and it was generally believed that Louis Lacombe, who was looked upon as an eccentric and whimsical young fellow, had gone abroad without acquainting any of his friends with his intentions.

If we accept this somewhat improbable suggestion, one question remains, a question of supreme importance to the country: what became of the plans of the submarine? Did Louis Lacombe take them with him? Were they destroyed?

We have caused the most serious investigations to be made, resulting in the conclusion that the plans are in existence. The brothers Varin have had them in their hands. How did they obtain possession of them? This we have not yet succeeded in establishing, any more than we know why they did not try to sell them sooner. They may have feared lest they should be asked whence they obtained them. In any case, this fear subsided in course of time, and we are in a position to state as a certainty that Louis Lacombe's plans are now the property of a foreign power, and, if necessary, to publish the letters exchanged in this connection between the representatives of that power and the brothers Varin. At the moment of writing the Seven of Hearts conceived by Louis Lacombe has been brought into actual existence by our neighbours.

Will the reality answer to the optimistic expectations of the men implicated in this act of treason? We have reasons for hoping the contrary, and we should like to think that these reasons will be justified by the event.

And a postscript added:

Our hopes were well grounded. Private information received at the moment of going to press enables us to state that the trials of the Seven of Hearts have not proved satisfactory. It is quite probable that the plans delivered by the Varins lacked the last document which Louis Lacombe brought to M. Andermatt, on the evening of his disappearance, a document which was essential to the complete understanding of the project — a sort of summary of definite conclusions, valuations and measurements contained in the other papers. Without this document the plans remain imperfect, even as the document is useless without the plans.

There is, therefore, still time to take action and to recover what belongs to us. In undertaking this very difficult task we rely greatly upon the assistance of M. Andermatt. He will be anxious to explain the apparently inexplicable conduct which he has maintained from the first. He will say not only why he did not tell what he knew at the time of Etienne Varin's suicide, but also why he never mentioned the disappearance of the papers with the existence of which he was acquainted. He will also say why, for the past six years, he has had the brothers Varin watched by detectives in his pay.

We look to him for deeds, not words. If not . . .

The article ended with this brutal implied threat. But what force did it possess? What means of intimidation could 'Salvator,' the anonymous writer of the article, hope to exercise over M. Andermatt?

A host of reporters swept down on the banker, and a dozen interviews described the scorn with which he rejected the insinuations which seemed to bring the matter home to him. Thereupon the correspondent of the Echo de France retorted with these three lines:

'M. Andermatt may like it or dislike it, but from to-day he is our collaborator in the work which we have undertaken.'

On the day when this rejoinder appeared Daspry and I dined together. After dinner, with the newspapers spread out on my table before us, we discussed the case, and went into it from every point of view, with the irritation which a man would feel if he were walking indefinitely in the dark, and constantly stumbling over the same obstacles.

Suddenly — for the bell had not rung — the door opened, and a lady covered with a thick veil, entered unannounced.

I at once rose to meet her. She said:

'Are you the gentleman that lives here?'

'Yes, madame. But I am bound to say . . . '

'The gate on the boulevard was open,' she explained.

'But the hall door? . . . '

She made no reply, and I reflected that she

must have gone round by the tradesmen's entrance. Then she knew the way?

A rather embarrassing pause ensued. She looked at Daspry. I introduced him to her mechanically — as I would have done in a drawing-room. Then I offered her a chair, and asked her to tell me the object of her visit.

She raised her veil, and I saw that she was dark, with regular features, and that, though not very pretty, she possessed an infinite charm, which came, above all, from her eyes — her grave, sad eyes.

She said simply:

'I am Madame Andermatt.'

'Madame Andermatt!' I repeated, more and more surprised.

There was a fresh pause. And she resumed, in a calm voice and an exceedingly quiet manner:

'I have come about that matter . . . which you know of. I thought that perhaps you might be able to give me some particulars . . . '

'Upon my word, Madame, I know no more about it than what has appeared in the papers. Please tell me precisely how I can be of use to you.'

'I don't know . . . I don't know . . . '

It was only then that I received an intuition that her calmness was assumed, and that a great agitation lay hidden under this air of perfect security. And we were silent, both equally embarrassed.

But Daspry, who had never ceased watching her, came up to her, and said:

'Will you allow me to put a few questions to you, Madame?'

'Oh yes!' she cried. 'I will speak if you do that.'

'You will speak . . . whatever the questions may be?'

'Whatever they may be.'

He reflected, and then asked:

'Did you know Louis Lacombe?'

'Yes, through my husband.'

'When did you see him last?'

'On the evening when he dined with us.'

'On that evening did nothing lead you to think that you would never see him again?'

'No. He said something about a journey to Russia, but it was a vague allusion.'

'So you expected to see him soon?'

'Yes, the next day but one, at dinner.'

'And how do you account for his disappearance?'

'I can't account for it.'

'And Monsieur Andermatt?'

'I don't know.'

'Still . . . '

'Don't ask me about that.'

'The article in the Echo de France seems to suggest . . . '

'What it seems to suggest is that the brothers Varin had something to do with his disappearance.'

'Is that your own opinion?'

'Yes.'

'On what do you base your conviction?'

'When Louis Lacombe left us he was carrying a portfolio containing all the papers relating to his scheme. Two days later my husband and one of the Varins, the one who is still alive, had an interview, in the course of which my husband acquired the certainty that those papers were in the hands of the two brothers.'

'And did he not lodge an information?'

'No.'

'Why not?'

'Because there was something in the portfolio besides Louis Lacombe's papers.'

'What was that?'

She hesitated, made as though to answer, and, finally, kept silence. Daspry continued:

'So that is the reason why your husband had the two brothers watched without informing the police. He hoped to recover both the papers and that other . . . compromising thing, thanks to which the two brothers levied a sort of blackmail on him.'

'On him . . . and on me.'

'Ah, on you, too?'

'On me principally.'

She uttered these three words in a dull voice. Daspry observed her, took a few steps aside, and, returning to her:

'Did you write to Louis Lacombe?'

'Certainly . . . my husband had business . . . '

'Apart from those official letters, did you not write Louis Lacombe . . . any other letters? . . . Forgive me for insisting, but it is essential that I should know the whole truth. Did you write any other letters?'

She turned very red, and murmured:

'Yes.'

'And are those the letters which the brothers Varin had in their possession?'

'Yes.'

'So Monsieur Andermatt knows?'

'He never saw them, but Alfred Varin told him of their existence, and threatened to publish them if my husband took action. My husband was afraid . . . he dreaded a scandal.'

'Only he did all he could to obtain the letters from them.'

'He did all he could . . . at least, I presume so; for ever since the day of that last interview with Alfred Varin, and after the few very violent words in which he told me of it, there has been no intimacy, no confidence between my husband and myself. We live together like two strangers.'

'In that case, if you have nothing to lose, what do you fear?'

'However indifferent I may have become to him, I am the woman he once loved, the woman he could still have loved — oh, I am certain of that!' she whispered, in an eager voice. 'He would still have loved me if he had not obtained possession of those accursed letters.'

'What! Did he succeed? . . . But surely the two brothers were on their guard?'

'Yes; and it seems that they even used to boast of having a safe hiding-place.'

'Well? . . . '

'I have reason to believe that my husband has discovered the hiding-place.'

'Not really! Where was it?'

'Here.'

I started.

'Here!'

'Yes; and I always suspected it. Louis Lacombe, who was very clever and had a passion for mechanics, used to amuse himself, in his spare time, by constructing locks and safes. The brothers Varin must have discovered one of these receptacles, and used it afterwards for the purpose of hiding the letters . . . and other things as well, no doubt.'

'But they did not live here!' I exclaimed.

'This house stood empty until your arrival, four months ago. They probably, therefore, used to come here; and they will have thought, moreover, that your presence need not hinder them on the day when they might want to withdraw all their papers. But they reckoned without my husband, who, on the night of the twenty-second of June, forced the safe, took . . . what he was looking for, and left his card behind him to make it quite clear to the two brothers that the tables were turned, and that he no longer had any cause to fear them. Two days later, after seeing your article in the Gil Blas, Etienne Varin came to call on you in hot haste, was left alone in this room, found the safe empty . . . and shot himself.'

After a moment's silence, Daspry asked:

'This is a mere conjecture, is it not? Has Monsieur Andermatt said anything to you?'

'No.'

'Has his attitude towards you changed? Has he seemed to you to be brooding or betrayed any anxiety?'

'No.'

'And don't you think that he would, if he had found the letters? For my part, I don't believe that he has them. In my opinion, it was some one else who entered here.'

'But who can it have been?'

'The mysterious person who is managing this business, who holds all the threads of it, and who is directing it towards an object of which we can only catch a glimpse through all these complications; the mysterious person whose invisible and all-powerful action has been felt from the start. It was he and his friends who entered this house on the twenty-second of June; it was he who discovered the hiding-place; it was he who left Monsieur Andermatt's card behind him; it is he who has the correspondence of the brothers Varin and the proofs of their treason in his keeping.'

'But who is 'he'?' I broke in, with some impatience.

'Why, the correspondent of the Echo de France, of course — 'Salvator'. Isn't the evidence overpowering? Doesn't the article give details that could be known only to the man who had fathomed the secrets of the two brothers?'

'In that case,' stammered Madame Andermatt, in dismay, 'he has my letters as well, and he will threaten my husband in his turn! What, in Heaven's name, am I to do?'

'Write to him,' said Daspry, plainly. 'Confide in him straight out, tell him all that you know, and all that you can learn.'

'What!'

'Your interests and his are identical. It is beyond all question that he is acting against the survivor of the two brothers. He is seeking a weapon against Alfred Varin, not against Monsieur Andermatt. Help him.'

'How?'

'Has your husband that document which completes Louis Lacombe's plans and allows them to be employed?'

'Yes.'

'Tell 'Salvator' so. If need be, try to procure the document for him. In short, enter into correspondence with him. What risk do you run?'

The advice was daring, at first sight even dangerous, but Madame Andermatt had very little choice. Besides, as Daspry said, what was she risking? If the unknown individual was an enemy, this step rendered the situation no worse than before. If he was a stranger pursuing some private aim, he must attach but a secondary importance to those letters.

In any case, it was an idea; and Madame Andermatt, in her mental disarray, was only too pleased to fall in with it. She thanked us effusively, and promised to keep us informed.

Two days later she sent us a line which she had received in reply:

The letters were not there. But set your mind at rest: I shall have them.

I am attending to everything.

S

I took up the note. It was in the same handwriting as the communication which I had found in my bedside book on the evening of the twenty-second of June.

So Daspry was right: 'Salvator' was the great wire-puller in this affair.

★   ★   ★

We were beginning, in fact, to discern a few gleams amid the surrounding darkness, and certain points became illuminated with an unexpected light. But others remained obscure, such as the discovery of the two sevens of hearts. I, on my side, always harked back to this, being more puzzled, perhaps, than I need have been by those two cards whose seven pierced pips had struck my eyes in such perturbing circumstances. What part did they play in the drama? What importance were we to attribute to them? What conclusion were we to draw from the fact that the submarine built in accordance with Louis Lacombe's plans bore the name of the Seven of Hearts?

As for Daspry, he paid little attention to the two cards, but devoted himself entirely to the study of another problem, the solution of which struck him as more urgent: he hunted indefatigably for the famous hiding-place.

'Who knows,' he said, 'That I shall not succeed in finding the letters which Salvator failed to find . . . through inadvertence, perhaps? It seems hardly credible that the Varins should have removed from a place which they considered inaccessible the weapon of which they knew the inestimable value.'

And he went on hunting. Soon the big room had no secret left for him, and he extended his investigations to all the other rooms in the house, searched the inside and the outside, examined the stones and bricks of the walls, lifted up the slates of the roof.

One day he arrived with a pickaxe and a spade, gave me the spade, kept the pickaxe, and, pointing to the waste ground, said:

'Come along.'

I followed him without enthusiasm. He divided the ground into a number of sections, which he inspected in sequence, until, in one corner, at the angle formed by the walls of two adjoining properties, his attention was attracted by a heap of stones and rubble overgrown with brambles and grass. He attacked it forthwith.

I had to help him. For an hour we labored to no purpose in the glaring sun. But when, after removing the stones, we came to the ground itself and opened it, Daspry's pickaxe laid bare a number of bones — the remains of a skeleton with shreds of clothing still clinging to it.

And suddenly I felt myself turn pale. I saw, stuck into the earth, a small iron plate, cut in a rectangular shape, and seeming to bear some red marks. I stooped. It was as I thought: the iron plate was the size of a playing-card, and the marks, the colour of red corroded in places, were seven in number, arranged like the pips of a seven of hearts, and pierced with a hole at each of the seven points.

'Listen to me, Daspry,' I said. 'I've had enough of all this business. It's very pleasant for you, if it interests you. But I shall leave you to enjoy it by yourself.'

Was it the excitement? Was it the fatigue of a piece of work carried out in the heat of too fierce a sun? The fact remains that I staggered as I went, and that I had to take to my bed, where I remained for forty-eight hours in a burning fever, and obsessed by skeletons that danced around me and threw their blood-red hearts at one another's heads.

Daspry was faithful to me. Every day he gave me three or four hours of his time, though it is true that he spent them in ferreting, tapping, and poking around the big room.

'The letters are in there, in that room,' he came and told me, at intervals. 'They're in there. I'll stake my life on it.'

'Leave me alone, for goodness' sake,' I replied, with my hair standing on end.

★ ★ ★

On the morning of the third day I got up, feeling very weak still, but cured. A substantial lunch did me good. But an express letter which I received at about five o'clock contributed even more to my recovery and stimulated my curiosity anew, in spite of everything.

The letter contained these words:

SIR — The play of which the first act was performed on the night of the 22nd of June is approaching its conclusion. As the force of things requires that I should bring the two principal characters face to face, and that this the confrontation should take place at your

188

house, I shall be infinitely obliged if you will let me have the use of your house this evening. It would be a good thing if your servant could be sent out from nine to eleven, and perhaps it would be as well if you yourself would be so extremely kind as to leave the field free to the adversaries. You were able to see for yourself, on the 22nd of June, that I made a point of respecting all your belongings. I, for my part, would consider that I was insulting you if I were for a moment to doubt your absolute discretion with regard to
Yours sincerely,
SALVATOR.

I was delighted with the tone of courteous irony in which this letter was couched, and with the pretty wit of the request it conveyed. It was so charmingly free and unconstrained, and my correspondent seemed so sure of my compliance! I would not for the world have disappointed him or replied to his confidence with ingratitude.

My servant, to whom I had given a ticket for the theatre, was out at eight o'clock when Daspry arrived. I showed him the letter. He said:

'Well?'

'Well, I shall leave the garden gate unlocked, so that he can come in.'

'And are you going out?'

'Not if I know it!'

'But he asks you to . . . '

'He asks me to be discreet. I shall be discreet. But I am mad with curiosity to see what happens.'

Daspry laughed:

'By Jove, you're right; and I shall stay too. Something tells me that we sha'n't be bored . . . '

He was interrupted by a ring at the bell.

'Are they there already?' he said, quietly. 'Twenty minutes before their time? Impossible!'

I went to the hall, and pulled the cord that opened the garden gate. A woman's figure came down the path: it was Madame Andermatt.

She seemed greatly upset, and her voice caught as she stammered out:

'My husband . . . he's on his way . . . He has an appointment here . . . They're going to give him the letters . . . '

'How do you know?' I asked.

'By accident. My husband had a message during dinner.'

'An express letter?'

'No, the message was telephoned. The servant handed it to me by mistake. My husband took it from me at once, but it was too late . . . I had read it.'

'What did it say?'

'Something like this: 'Be at the Boulevard Maillot at nine this evening with the documents relating to the business. In exchange, the letters.' When dinner was over, I went up to my room and came on here.'

'Unknown to Monsieur Andermatt?'

'Yes.'

Daspry looked at me.

'What do you think of it?'

'I think what you think, that Monsieur Andermatt is one of the adversaries summoned.'

'By whom? And for what purpose?'

'That is exactly what we shall see.'

I took them to the big room. We found that there was just space for the three of us under the chimney-mantel, and that we could hide behind the velvet curtain. Madame Andermatt sat down between Daspry and myself. We had a view of the whole room through the slits in the hangings.

The clock struck nine. A few minutes later the garden gate grated on its hinges.

I confess that I felt a certain pang, and that a new fever seized upon me. I was on the point of discovering the key to the mystery! The bewildering adventure whose successive phases had been unfolding themselves before me for weeks was at last about to adopt its real meaning, and the battle was to be fought before my eyes.

Daspry took Madame Andermatt's hand, and whispered:

'Be sure that you do not make a movement. Whatever you see or hear, remain impassive.'

A man entered the room, and I at once recognized Alfred Varin by his strong resemblance to his brother Etienne. He had the same heavy gait, the same dark, bearded face.

He came in with the anxious air of a man who is accustomed to fear ambushes around him, who suspects them and avoids them. He cast a rapid glance all around the room, and I felt that that chimney hidden by a velvet curtain annoyed him. He took three steps in our direction. But an idea, doubtless more urgent than the first, diverted him from his intention; for, turning towards the wall, he stopped before the old mosaic emperor with the flowing beard and the gleaming sword, and examined the figure at length, mounting a chair, following the outline of the shoulders and the face with his finger, and touching certain portions as he did so.

But suddenly he jumped from his chair,

and moved away from the wall. A sound of footsteps approached. M. Andermatt appeared upon the threshold.

The banker uttered an exclamation of surprise.

'You! You! Was it you that sent for me?'

'I? Not at all!' protested Varin, in a grating voice that reminded me of his brother's. 'I came because of your letter.'

'My letter!'

'A letter signed by you, in which you offer me . . . '

'I never wrote to you.'

'You never wrote to me!'

Instinctively Varin took up a position of defence, not against the banker, but against the unknown foe who had drawn him into this snare. For the second time his eyes turned in our direction, and, with a quick step, he moved towards the door.

M. Andermatt blocked his way.

'What are you doing, Varin?'

'There's more in this than meets the eye. I don't like it. I'm going. Good-night.'

'One moment.'

'Come, Monsieur Andermatt, don't insist; you and I have nothing to say to each other.'

'We have a great deal to say to each other, and the opportunity is too good . . . '

'Let me pass.'

'No, no, no, you shall not pass.'

Varin fell back, cowed by the banker's resolute attitude, and mumbled:

'Be quick, then; say what you have to say, and be done with it!'

One thing astonished me, and I had no doubt that my two companions underwent the same feeling of disappointment. Why was 'Salvator' not there? Did it not form part of his plan to interfere? Did the mere bringing together of the banker and Varin appear to him enough? I felt curiously ill at ease. By the fact of 'Salvator's' absence, this duel, desired and contrived by himself, was assuming the tragic turn of an event created and controlled by the strict order of destiny; and the force that was now hurling these two men against each other was the more impressive inasmuch as it existed outside themselves.

After a moment M. Andermatt went up to Varin, and, standing right in front of him and looking him straight in the eyes, said:

'Now that the years have passed, and that you have nothing more to fear, answer me frankly, Varin. What have you done with Louis Lacombe?'

'There's a question! As if I could know what has become of him!'

'You do know! You do know! You and your brother followed his every footstep, you

194

almost lived with him in this very house where we are standing. You knew all about his work, all about his schemes. An on that last evening, Varin, when I saw Louis Lacombe to my front door, I caught sight of two figures lurking in the shadow. That I am prepared to swear to.'

'Well, and when you have sworn to it? . . . '

'It was your brother and you, Varin.'

'Prove it.'

'Why, the best proof is that, two days later, you yourself showed me the papers and plans which you had found in Lacombe's portfolio, and offered to sell them to me. How did those papers come into your possession?'

'I told you, Monsieur Andermatt, that we found them on Louis Lacombe's table the next morning after he had disappeared.'

'That's a lie.'

'Prove it.'

'The police could have proved it.'

'Why didn't you go to the police?'

'Why? Ah, why? . . . '

He was silent, with a gloomy face. And the other resumed:

'You see, Monsieur Andermatt, if you had the least certainty, you would not have allowed our little threat to prevent you . . . '

'What threat? Those letters? Do you imagine that I ever believed for a moment . . . ?'

'If you did not believe in those letters, why did you offer me untold money to give them up? And why, since then, did you have my brother and me hunted like wild beasts?'

'To recover the plans which I wanted.'

'Nonsense! You wanted the letters! Once in possession of the letters, you would have informed against us. You didn't catch me parting with them!' A sudden fit of laughter interrupted him. 'But enough of this. It's no use saying the same thing over and over again; we should get no further. So we'll drop the subject.'

'We will do nothing of the kind,' said the banker, 'and, now that you have spoken of the letters, you shall not go from this place without handing them over to me.'

'I shall go!'

'No, no, no!'

'Listen to me, Monsieur Andermatt: I advise you . . . '

'You shall not go.'

'We shall see,' said Varin, in so furious a tone that Madame Andermatt stifled a faint cry.

He must have heard it, for he tried to pass by force. M. Andermatt pushed him back violently. Then I saw him slip his hand into his jacket-pocket.

'For the last time!'

'The letters first.'

Varin drew a revolver, and, pointing it at M. Andermatt, said:

'Yes or no?'

The banker stooped quickly.

A shot rang out. The weapon fell to the ground.

I was dumbfounded. The shot had been fired from my side. And it was Daspry who, with a pistol bullet, had dashed the revolver out of Alfred Varin's hand!

Standing suddenly between the two adversaries, facing Varin, he sneered:

'You're lucky, my friend, you're jolly lucky! I aimed at your hand and hit your revolver.'

Both men stared at him in confusion. He said to the banker:

'Forgive me, sir, for interfering in what does not concern me. But really you play your cards very badly. Let me hold them for you.'

Turning to the other:

'Now, then, my lad; and play the game please. Hearts are trumps, and I lead the seven!'

And he banged the iron plate with the seven red pips within three inches of Varin's nose.

Never did I see a man so taken aback. Livid, his eyes starting from his head, his features distorted with agony, Varin seemed hypnotized by the sight before him.

'Who are you?' he stammered.

'I have already told you: a gentleman who meddles with what does not concern him . . . but who meddles with it to the bitter end.'

'What do you want?'

'All that you've brought.'

'I've brought nothing.'

'Yes, you have, or you wouldn't have come. You received a note this morning telling you to be here at nine o'clock, and to bring all the papers you had. Well, you're here. Where are the papers?'

There was an air of authority in Daspry's voice and attitude that nonplussed me, a pre-emptory demeanour that was quite new to me in this rather easy-going and mild-mannered man. Varin, now entirely subdued, pointed to one of his pockets:

'The papers are in there.'

'Are they all there?'

'Yes.'

'All that you found in Louis Lacombe's portfolio and sold to Major von Lieben?'

'Yes.'

'Are they the copies or the originals?'

'The originals.'

'What do you want for them?'

'A hundred thousand francs.'

Daspry burst out:

'You're mad! The major only gave you twenty thousand. Twenty thousand francs flung away, now that the trials have failed.'

'They did not know how to use the plans.'

'The plans are not complete.'

'Then why do you ask for them?'

'I want them. I'll give you five thousand francs. Not a sou more.'

'Ten thousand. Not a sou less.'

Daspry turned to M. Andermatt.

'Be good enough, sir, to sign a cheque.'

'But . . . I haven't my . . .'

'Your cheque-book? Here it is.'

Astounded, M. Andermatt fingered the cheque-book which Daspry handed him.

'It's my cheque-book . . . But how . . . ?'

'My dear sir, please don't waste words: you have only to fill it in.'

The banker took out his stylograph, and filled in and signed the cheque. Varin held out his hand.

'Paws off!' said Daspry. 'We're not done yet.'

And to the banker:

'There was a question also of some letters which you claim.'

'Yes, a bundle of letters.'

'Where are they, Varin?'

'I haven't them.'

'Where are they, Varin?'

'I don't know. My brother took charge of them.'

'They are hidden here, in this room.'

'In that case, you know where they are.'

'How should I know?'

'Considering it was you that went to the hiding-place! You seem to be as well informed as . . . 'Salvator'!'

'The letters are not in the hiding-place.'

'They are.'

'Open it.'

A look of distrust passed over Varin's face. Were Daspry and 'Salvator' really one, as everything led him to presume? If so, he risked nothing by revealing a hiding-place that was already known. If not, there was no point in . . .

'Open it,' repeated Daspry.

'I haven't a seven of hearts.'

'Yes, here's one,' said Daspry, holding out the iron plate.

Varin fell back in terror.

'No . . . no . . . I will not . . . '

'Never mind that . . . '

Daspry went up to the old emperor with the flowing beard, climbed a chair, and applied the seven of hearts to the bottom of the sword, against the hilt, so that the edges of the plate exactly covered the two edges of the blade. The, with the point of an awl, which he pressed successively through each of the seven holes contrived in the end of the seven pips, he pressed upon seven of the tiny stones composing the mosaic. When the seventh stone was driven in, a catch was released, and the whole of the emperor's bust turned on a pivot, revealing a wide aperture arranged as a safe, iron-cased and fitted with two shelves of gleaming steel.

'You see, Varin, the safe is empty.'

'Just so . . . Then my brother must have removed the letters.'

Daspry came back to the man, and said:

'Don't try to get the better of me. There is another hiding-place. Where is it?'

'There isn't one.'

'Is it money you want? How much?'

'Ten thousand francs.'

'Monsieur Andermatt, are those letters worth ten thousand francs to you?'

'Yes,' said the banker, in a firm voice.

Varin shut the safe, took the seven of hearts, not without a visible repugnance, and applied it to the blade, at exactly the same place, against the hilt. He drove the awl successively through the end of the seven pips. There was a second release of a catch, but, this time, an unexpected thing occurred:

only a part of the safe turned round, disclosing a smaller safe, contrived in the thickness of the door that closed the large one.

The bundle of letters was there, tied up with tape and sealed. Varin gave it to Daspry, who asked:

'Is the cheque ready, Monsieur Andermatt?'

'Yes.'

'And have you also the last document, which Louis Lacombe left with you, completing the plans of the submarine?'

'Yes.'

The exchange was made. Daspry pocketed the document and the cheque, and offered the packet to M. Andermatt.

'Here is what you wanted, sir.'

The banker hesitated a moment, as though he were afraid to touch those cursed pages which he had been so eager to find. Then he took them, with a nervous movement.

I heard a groan by my side. I caught hold of Madame Andermatt's hand; it was icy cold.

And Daspry said to the banker:

'I think, sir, that our conversation is ended. Oh, no thanks, I beg of you. It was a mere accident that enabled me to serve you.'

M. Andermatt withdrew, taking with him

his wife's letters to Louis Lacombe.

'Splendid!' cried Daspry, with an air of delight. 'Everything is arranged for the best. You and I have only to settle our business, my lad. Have you the papers?'

'They are all here.'

Daspry looked through them, examined them closely, and stuffed them into his pocket.

'Quite right; you have kept your word.'

'But . . . '

'But what?'

'The two cheques? . . . The money? . . . '

'Well, you're a cool hand, you are! What! You dare put in a claim . . . '

'I claim what is owed me.'

'Do you mean to say that you're owed anything for papers which you stole?'

But the man was beside himself. He shook with rage; his eyes were shot with blood.

'Give me my money . . . the twenty thousand francs,' he stuttered.

'Out of the question . . . I appropriate it.'

'My money!'

'Come, be reasonable . . . and drop that dagger, will you?'

He caught him by the arm so roughly that the other roared with pain. And he added:

'Go away, my lad, the air will do you good. Would you like me to see you off? We will go by the waste ground, and I will show you a heap of stones and brambles under which . . . '

'It's not true! It's not true!'

'Yes, it is true. This little iron plate with the seven pips came from there. Louis Lacombe used to always carry it about with him, don't you remember? You and your brother buried it with the corpse . . . and with other things which will interest the police enormously.'

Varin covered his face with his raging fists. Then he said:

'Very well. I have been done. Let's say no more about it. One word, however . . . just one word . . . I want to know . . . '

'I am listening . . . '

'There was a cash-box in that safe, in the larger of the two.'

'Yes.'

'Was it there when you came here on the night of the twenty-second of June?'

'Yes.'

'What was inside it?'

'All that the brothers Varin had locked up in it: a pretty collection of jewels, diamonds, and pearls, picked up right and left by the brothers aforesaid.'

'And did you take it?'

'By Jove! what would you have done in my place?'

'Then ... it was after he discovered the disappearance of the cash-box that my brother committed suicide?'

'Probably.' The disappearance of your correspondence with Major van Lieben would hardly have been enough. But the cash-box was another matter ... Is that all you wanted to know?'

'One thing more: your name?'

'You say that as though you were thinking of revenge.'

'Quite right! One's luck turns. You're on top today. To-morrow ... '

'You may be.'

'I hope so. What's your name?'

'Arsène Lupin.'

'Arsène Lupin!'

The man staggered back as though he had received a blow on the head with a club. Those two words seemed to dash all his hopes. Daspry laughed.

'Ah, so you thought that some Monsieur Durand or Dupont had managed this fine business? Come, come, it must have needed an Arsène Lupin at least. And now that you know all you wanted to, old chap, go and prepare your revenge. You will find Arsène Lupin waiting for you.'

And without another word, he pushed him out of the door.

'Daspry, Daspry!' I cried, still, in spite of myself, calling him by the name by which I had known him.

I pulled back the velvet curtain.

He ran up.

'What is it? What's the matter?'

'Madame Andermatt is fainting.'

He hastened up, made her sniff at a bottle of salts, and, while he was bringing her round, asked:

'Well, but what happened?'

'The letters,' I said. 'The letters which you gave her husband.'

He struck his forehead.

'What! She believed ... But, after all, why shouldn't she believe? ... Fool that I am!'

Madame Andermatt, when she had recovered consciousness, listened to him greedily. He drew from his pocket a little bundle similar in every respect to that which M. Andermatt had taken away with him.

'Here are your letters, Madame — the real ones.'

'But ... the others?'

'The others are like these, but were copied out by me last night, and carefully altered. Your husband will be all the better pleased when he reads them, as he has no idea that they are not the originals.'

'But the writing . . . '

'There is no writing that can't be imitated.'

She thanked him in the same terms of gratitude which she would have addressed to a man of her own station, and it was clear to me that she could not have heard the last sentences exchanged between Varin and Arsène Lupin.

As for myself, I looked at him with a certain perplexity, not quite knowing what to say to this old friend who was revealing himself to me in so unexpected a light. But Lupin, very much at his ease, said:

'You can say good-bye to Jean Daspry.'

'Really!'

'Yes, Jean Daspry is going abroad. I am sending him to Morocco, where he will probably come to an end quite worthy of him; in fact, he has made up his mind.'

'But Arsène Lupin remains . . . ?'

'I should think so! Arsène Lupin is only at the beginning of his career, and he fully means to . . . '

An impulse of irresistible curiosity attracted me to him, and, leading him to some distance from Madame Andermatt, I asked:

'So you ended by discovering the second hiding-place containing the letters?'

'It took me long enough, though! It was not until yesterday afternoon while you were still in bed. And yet goodness knows how easy it was! But the simplest things always occur to one last.' And showing me the seven of hearts: 'I had guessed that, to open the large safe, one had to rest this card against the sword of the old boy in mosaic . . . '

'How did you guess that?'

'Easily. From private information, I knew, when I came here, on the evening of the twenty-second of June . . . '

'After leaving me . . . '

'Yes; and after selecting my conversation so as to throw you into such a state of mind that a nervous and impressionable man like yourself was bound to let me act as I pleased without leaving his bed.'

'The reasoning was sound.'

'Well, I knew when I came here that there was a cash-box hidden in a safe with a secret lock, to which the seven of hearts formed the key. It was only a question of applying the seven of hearts to a place that was obviously intended for it. An hour's examination was enough for me.'

'An hour!'

'Look at the old boy in mosaic.'

'The emperor?'

'That old emperor is the exact image of Charlemagne, who figures as the king of hearts in every French pack.'

'You're quite right . . . But why should the seven of hearts open sometimes the large safe and sometimes the small one? And why did you open only the large safe at first?'

'Why?' Because I persisted in always applying my seven of hearts in the same way. Yesterday only I perceived that, by turning it round — that is to say, by putting the seventh pip, the middle one, with its point up instead of down — the position of the seven pips was altered.'

'Of course.'

'It's easy to say 'of course,' but I ought to have thought of it.'

'Another thing: you knew nothing about the story of the letters until Madame Andermatt . . . '

'Spoke of it before me? Just so. I found nothing in the safe besides the cash-box, except the correspondence of the two brothers, which put me on the scent of their treason.'

'So, when all is said, it was chance that made you first reconstruct the history of the two brothers, and next search for the plans and documents of the submarine?'

'Pure chance.'

'But what was your object in making those researches? . . . '

Daspry interrupted me with a laugh.

'Bless my soul, how the thing interests you!'

'It interests me, madly.'

'Well, presently, when I have seen Madame Andermatt home and sent a messenger to the Echo de France with a few lines which I want to write, I will come back, and we will go into details.'

He sat down and wrote one of those monumental little paragraphs that delight his whimsical imagination. Who does not remember the noise which this particular one made throughout the world:

'Arsène Lupin has solved the problem which was set the other day by 'Salvator.' He has obtained possession of all the original plans and documents of Louis Lacombe, the engineer, and has forwarded them to the Minister of Marine. Moreover, Arsène Lupin is opening subscription to present the state with the first submarine constructed after these plans. And he himself has headed the list by subscribing twenty thousand francs.'

'The twenty thousand francs of the Andermatt cheques?' I said, when he had given me the paper to read.

'Exactly. It was only fair that Varin should at least partly redeem his treason.'

★ ★ ★

210

And that was how I came to know Arsène Lupin. That was how I learned that Jean Daspry, my acquaintance at the club and in society, was none other than Arsène Lupin, the gentleman-burglar. That was how I formed bonds of a very pleasant friendship with the great man, and how, thanks to the confidence with which he deigns to honour me, I gradually came to be his most humble, devoted, and grateful biographer.

Madame Imbert's Safe

It was three o'clock in the morning, and there were still some half-dozen carriages in front of one of those little artist's houses which form the one and only side of the Boulevard Berthier. The door opened. A group of guests, men and women, came out into the street. Four carriages drove off to right and left, and there remained upon the pavement only two gentlemen, who parted company at the corner of the Rue de Courcelles, where one of them lived. The other decided to go home to the Porte-Maillot on foot.

He therefore crossed the Avenue de Villiers and continued his road on the side opposite the fortifications. He found it pleasant walking in this bright and frosty winter night. The sound of his footsteps echoed gaily as he went.

But after some minutes he began to have the disagreeable impression that he was being followed; and, in fact, on turning round he perceived the shadow of a man gliding between the trees. He was not of a nervous disposition; nevertheless, he hastened his steps in order to reach the Octroi des Ternes as quickly as possible. But the man behind him broke into a run; and, feeling more or less anxious, he thought it better to face him and to take his revolver from his pocket.

He did not have time to complete his purpose. The man attacked him violently, and then and there a fight commenced on the deserted boulevard — a fight at close quarters in which he at once felt that he had the disadvantage. He shouted for help, struggled and was knocked down upon a heap of flint-stones, caught up by the throat and gagged with a handkerchief, which his adversary stuffed into his mouth. His eyes closed, his ears buzzed, and he was on the point of losing consciousness when suddenly the pressure was relieved, and the man who had been stifling him with the weight of his body rose to defend himself in his turn against an unexpected attack.

A blow on the wrist from a walking-stick, a kick on the ankle, and the man gave two groans of pain and ran away, limping and swearing as he went.

Without condescending to go in pursuit, the newcomer stooped and asked:

'Are you hurt, sir?'

The victim was not hurt, but quite dazed and unable to stand. As luck would have it, one of the officials of the Octroi, attracted by the shouts, came hastening up. A cab was hailed, and the gentleman stepped into it, accompanied by his rescuer, and was driven to his house in the Avenue de la Grande-Armée.

On arriving at his door, now quite recovered, he was lost in thanks.

'I owe you my life, sir, and you may be sure that I shall never forget it. I do not wish to alarm my wife at this time of night, but I want her to thank you herself before the day is out.'

He begged the other to come to lunch, and told him his name — Ludovic Imbert; adding:

'May I know to whom I have the honour . . . ?'

'Certainly,' said the other, introducing himself: 'Arsène Lupin.'

★ ★ ★

At that time — this was five years ago — Arsène Lupin had not yet attained the celebrity which he owed to the Cahorn case, his escape from the Santé, and a number of other resounding exploits. He was not even called Arsène Lupin. This name, for which the future held such a brilliant renown in store, was specially invented to denote M.

Imbert's rescuer, who may be said to have won his spurs in this encounter. Ready for the fray, it is true, armed at all points, but without resources, without the authority which success leads, Arsène was but an apprentice in a profession of which he was, erelong, to become a past-master.

It was only natural that he should feel an emotion of delight when he woke up and remembered the invitation of the night before. The goal was within reach at last! At last he was undertaking a work worthy of his powers and of his talent! The Imbert millions: what a magnificent prey for an appetite such as his!

He made a special toilet: a threadbare frock-coat, shabby trousers, a rusty silk hat, frayed shirt-collar and cuffs, the whole very clean, but having all the appearance of poverty. Thus dressed out, he walked down the staircase of his lodgings at Montmartre. On reaching the third floor, without stopping he tapped at a closed door with the knob of his walking-stick. Leaving the house, he made for the outer boulevards. A tram-car passed. He jumped into it, and a man who had been walking behind him, the occupant of the third floor, promptly took the seat beside him.

After a moment the man said:

'Well, governor?'

'Well, it's done.'

'How do you mean?'

'I'm lunching there.'

'You're lunching there?'

'You wouldn't have me risk a life as precious as mine for nothing, I hope? I have snatched M. Ludovic Imbert from the certain death which you had prepared for him. Monsieur Ludovic Imbert has a very grateful nature. He has asked me to lunch.'

A silence; and then the other ventured:

'So you're not giving it up?'

'My boy,' said Arsène, 'after plotting that little assault of last night, after taking the trouble, at three o'clock in the morning, along the fortifications, to give you a bank on the wrist and a kick on the shin and running the risk of inflicting personal damage of my one and only friend, it's not likely that I should give up the profits arising from a rescue so carefully planned.'

'But the unfavourable reports circulating about the fortune . . . '

'Let them circulate! It is six months since I first took the matter in hand; six months since I began to collect information, to study the case, to lay my snares, to question the servants, the moneylenders, and the men of straw; six months since I started shadowing the husband and wife. I don't care whether the fortune proceeds from old Rawford, as they contend, or from another source; but I declare that it exists. And, as it exists, I mean to have it.'

'Fichtre! A hundred millions!'

'Say ten, or even five — no matter! There are fat bundles of securities in the safe. I'll be hanged if I don't, sooner or later, lay hands on the key!'

The car stopped at the Place de l'Etoille.

'So, for the present . . . ?'

'Nothing to be done. I'll let you know. There's plenty of time.'

Five minutes later Arsène Lupin climbed the sumptuous staircase of the Hotel Imbert, and Ludovic introduced him to his wife. Gervaise was a nice little woman, round as a ball, and very talkative. She gave him the warmest of greetings.

'We wanted to be by ourselves to entertain our rescuer,' she said.

And from the first they treated 'our rescuer' as a friend of long standing. By the time that dessert was reached the intimacy was complete, and confidences were being exchanged at a great pace. Arsène told the story of his own life and the life of his father, an upright magistrate, described his sad childhood, his present difficulties. Gervaise, in her turn, talked of her youth, her marriage, old Rawford's kindnesses, the hundred millions which she had inherited, the obstacles that delayed her entering into their enjoyment, the loans which she had had to raise at exorbitant rates of interest, her endless strife with Rawford's nephews. And the injunctions! And the sequestrations! In fact, the whole story!

'Just think, Monsieur Lupin, the bonds are there, in the next room, in my husband's office, and if we cut off a single coupon we lose everything! There securities are there, in our safe, and we cannot touch them!'

A thrill passed through M. Lupin's frame at the thought of this proximity, and he felt very clearly that he would never have the problem of having the same scruples as the worthy lady.

'Ah, they are in there!' he murmured, with a parched throat. 'They are in there.'

Relations begun under such auspices as these were bound to lead to closer ties still. In reply to questions delicately worded, Arsène Lupin confessed his poverty, his distress. The poor fellow received his appointment, then and there, as private secretary to the pair, at a salary of one hundred and fifty francs a month. He was to go on living where he was, but to come every morning and receive his instructions for the day's work. For his greater comfort, a room on the second floor was placed at his disposal as a study.

He chose one for himself. By what stroke of luck did it happen to be immediately over Ludovic's office?

It did not take Arsène long to perceive that his secretaryship bore a furious resemblance to a sinecure. In two months he was given only four insignificant letters to copy out, and was only once called to his employer's office, which permitted him only once to catch an official glimpse of the safe. He noted, besides, that the titular of this sinecure was not even deemed worthy of figuring beside Anquety the deputy, or Grouvel the leader of the bar, for he was never invited to the famous fashionable receptions.

He did not complain, for he much preferred to keep to his modest little place in the shade. Nor did he waste time. From the first he paid a certain number of clandestine visits to Ludovic's office and presented his duty to the safe, which remained none the less hermetically sealed. The safe was a huge mass of cast-iron and steel, presenting a surly and stubborn appearance, and neither file nor crowbar could prevail against it.

Arsène Lupin was not an obstinate man.

'Where force fails, craft prevails,' he said.

'The great thing is to keep one's eyes and ears open.'

He took the necessary measurements, and, after much careful and difficult boring, inserted through the floor of his room a piece of lead pipe, which came out in the office ceiling, between two projections in the cornice.[1] Through this pipe, which served as both a speaking-tube and a spy-glass, he hoped to hear and see.

Thenceforward he spent his days lying flat on the floor of his room. And, as a matter of fact, he often saw the Imberts in close conference before the safe, turning up books and handling bundles of papers. When they twisted in succession the four knobs that worked the lock, he tried, in order to learn the code, to catch the number of notches that were passed. He watched their movements, listened to their words. What did they do with the key? Did they hide it somewhere?

One day he ran hurriedly downstairs, having seen them leave the room without locking the safe. He boldly entered the office.

---

[1] Author's note: In the course of the alterations affected by the Tourist Club, which, as the reader knows, was the purchaser of the Hotel Imbert, this pipe was discovered by the workmen, who were, of course, unable to explain its purpose.

They had returned.

'Oh, I beg your pardon, I made a mistake in the door . . . '

But Gervaise ran up to him and drew him into the room.

'Come in, Monsieur Lupin,' she said, 'don't you feel at home here? Come in and advise us. Which do you think we ought to sell out? Foreigners or Rentes?'

'But what about the injunction?' asked Lupin, greatly astonished.

'Oh, it does not affect all of the securities.'

She flung open the door of the safe. The shelves were heaped up with portfolios fastened with straps. She took out one of them. But her husband protested:

'No, no, Gervaise, it would be madness to sell foreign stock! It is going up . . . But the Rentes are as high as they are likely to go. What do you think, my dear fellow?'

The dear fellow had no opinion on the subject; however, he advised the sacrifice of the Rentes. Thereupon she caught hold of another file of papers, and from this file took a document at random. It was a bond in the Three-per-Cents. Ludovic put it in his pocket. In the afternoon, accompanied by his secretary, he took the bond to a broker to sell, and received forty-six thousand francs for it.

In spite of what Gervaise had said, Arsène

Lupin did not feel at home. On the contrary, his position in the Hotel Imbert filled him with surprise. He realized with a shock that the servants did not even know his name. They spoke of him as 'monsieur'. Ludovic always referred to him as such.

'You will tell monsieur . . . Has monsieur arrived yet?'

Why this enigmatical designation?

Moreover, after the first enthusiasm, the Imberts hardly spoke to him, and, while treating him with the consideration due to a benefactor, took no further notice of him at all! They appeared to look upon him as an eccentric who did not wish to be intruded on, and they respected his isolation as though this isolation had been a rule laid down by himself, a whim of his own. Once, as he was passing through the hall, he heard Gervaise remark to two gentleman:

'He's so shy!'

'Very well,' he thought, 'I'm shy.'

And he ceased to worry his head about the oddities of these people, and pursued the execution of his plan. He had acquired the certainty that it was no use relying upon chance or upon any act of thoughtlessness on the part of Gervaise, who never let the key out of her possession, and who, besides, never took away the key without first mixing up the mechanisms of the lock. He must, therefore, act for himself.

One thing hastened matters, which was the violent campaign conducted against the Imberts by a section of the press. They were accused of swindling. Arsène Lupin followed the evolutions of the drama and the consequent excitement in the household, and he understood that if he waited much longer he would lose all.

On five days in succession, instead of leaving at six o'clock, as was his habit, he locked himself into his room. He was supposed to have gone out. Stretched at full length on the floor he watched Ludovic's office.

On the sixth day, as the favourable circumstance for which he was waiting had not occurred, he went away in the middle of the night by the little door in the court-yard, of which he had a key.

But on the seventh day he learned that the Imberts, by way of replying to the malevolent insinuations of their enemies, had offered to publicly open the safe.

'It's to-night or never,' thought Lupin.

And, in fact, after dinner Ludovic went to his office accompanied by Gervaise. They began to turn over the pages of the books in the safe.

An hour passed, another hour. He heard the servants going up to bed. Now there was no one left on the first floor. Midnight struck. The Imberts went on with their work.

'Come on,' muttered Lupin.

He opened his window. It looked out upon the courtyard, and the space, on this moonless, starless night, was dark. He took from his cupboard a knotted rope, fastened it to the railing of the balcony, stepped over, and let himself down gently, with the help of a rain-spout, to the window beneath his own. It was the window of the office, and the thick curtains veiled the interior from his eyes. He stood for a moment motionless, listening carefully, on the balcony.

Reassured by the silence, he gave a slight push to the casement windows. If no one had checked them, they ought to yield to the slightest pressure, for, in the course of the afternoon, he had twisted the fastening in such a way as to prevent it from entering the staples.

The casements gave way. Thereupon, with infinite precautions, he opened them a little farther. As soon as he was able to pass his head through he stopped. A gleam of light filtered out between the curtains, which did not quite meet. He saw Gervaise and Ludovic sitting beside the safe.

Absorbed in their work, they exchanged but a few occasional words in a low voice. Arsène calculated the distance that separated him from them, settled upon the exact movements that would be necessary to reduce them to a state of helplessness, one after the other, before they had time to call for help, and was about to rush in upon them, when Gervaise said:

'How cold the room has turned! I am going to bed. Are you coming?'

'I should like to finish first.'

'Finish! Why, it will take you all night!'

'Oh no; an hour at the most.'

She went away. Twenty minutes, thirty minutes elapsed. Arsène pushed the window a little more. The curtains shook. He pushed still farther. Ludovic turned around, and, seeing the curtains swollen by the wind, rose to shut the window . . .

There was not a cry, not even the appearance of a struggle. With a few accurate movements and without doing Ludovic the least harm, Arsène stunned him, wrapped his head in the curtain, and tied him up so that he was not even able to distinguish his assailant's features.

Then he went quickly to the safe, took two portfolios, which he put under his arm, left the office, went down the stairs, crossed the courtyard, and opened the door of the servants' entrance. A cab was waiting in the street.

'Take these first,' he said to the driver, 'and come with me.'

They went back to the office. In two journeys they emptied the safe. Then Arsène went up to his room, hoisted in the rope, removed all traces of his passage. The thing was done.

A few hours after, Arsène Lupin, assisted by his companion, stripped the portfolios of their contents. He felt no disappointment, having foreseen as much, on ascertaining that the fortune of the Imberts was not as great as the rumours had ascribed to it. The millions did not number hundreds, or even tens. But, at any rate, the total made up a very respectable sum, and consisted of excellent securities: railway debentures, municipal loans, state funds, northern mines, and so on.

He declared himself satisfied:

'No doubt,' he said, 'there will be a sad loss when the time comes for dealing. There will be all sorts of difficulties, and I shall often have to let things go very cheap. Never mind! With this first capital, I undertake to live according to my ideas . . . and to realize a few dreams that lie near my heart.'

'And the rest?'

'Burn them, my lad. These piles of papers looked very well in the safe. They're no use to us. As for the securities, we'll lock them up in the cupboard, and wait calmly till the auspicious moment arrives to dispose of them.'

The next morning Arsène could see no reason why he should not return to the Hotel Imbert. But the papers contained an unexpected piece of news: Ludovic and Gervaise had disappeared.

The safe was opened amid great solemnity. The magistrates found what Arsène had left behind, an empty safe.

* * *

Such are the facts and such is the explanation of some of the details, owing to the intervention of Arsène Lupin. I had the story from his own lips one day when he was in a confidential vein.

He was walking up and down my study, and his eyes wore a little feverish look which I had never seen in them before.

'On the whole, therefore,' I said, 'this is your master-stroke.'

Without giving a direct answer, he continued:

'There are impenetrable secrets in this

business. Even after the explanation which I have given you a number of mysteries remain unsolved. For instance, why that flight? Why did they not take advantage of the assistance which I had involuntarily rendered them? It would have been so simple to say, The millions were there in the safe. They are not there now because they have been stolen.'

'They lost their nerve.'

'Yes, that's it, they lost their nerve . . . And yet, it is true . . . '

'What is true?'

'Oh, never mind.'

What did this reticence mean? He had not told me all, that was obvious; and what he had not told me he disliked telling. I was puzzled. The thing must be serious to provoke hesitation in a man of his stamp.

I put a few questions to him at haphazard.

'Did you never see them again?'

'No.'

'And did it never occur to you to feel any pity for those poor wretches?'

'I?' he cried, with a start.

His excitement astonished me. Had I hit the mark? I said:

'Of course. But for you, they might have stayed and faced the music . . . or at least gone off with their pockets filled.'

'So you expect me to feel remorse — is that it?'

'Well, in a sense.'

He struck the table with his clenched fist.

'So, according to you, I ought to feel remorse!'

'You can call it remorse, or regret, a feeling of some kind . . . '

'A feeling of some kind for that couple . . . '

'For a couple whom you robbed of a fortune.'

'What fortune?'

'Well . . . those two or three bundles of securities . . . '

'Those two or three bundles of securities! I robbed them of bundles of securities, did I? Part of their legacy, their fortune? Is that what I did? Is that my crime? But, bless my soul, my dear chap, haven't you guessed that those securities were so many forgeries? . . . Do you hear? They were forgeries!'

I looked at him, dumbfounded.

'What! those four or five millions were forgeries! . . . '

'Forgeries!' he shouted, in his rage, 'forgeries! every scrap: the debentures, the municipal loans, the state funds; not worth the paper they were printed on! Not a sou, not a single sou did I get out of the whole lot! And you ask me to feel remorse! But it's they who ought to feel remorse! They cheated me like a common jay! They plucked me like the meanest of their pigeons and the stupidest!'

He shook with a perfectly genuine anger, made up of personal resentment and wounded pride.

'Don't you see that they had the better of me from first to last, from start to finish? Do you know what part I played in the business, or rather what part they made me play? I was Andrew Rawford! Yes, my dear fellow, and I was completely taken in! I only learned it after reading the newspapers and comparing certain details. While I was posing as the benefactor, as the gentleman who had risked his life to save Imbert from the hooligans, he was passing me off as one of the Rawfords! Isn't it admirable? That eccentric who had his room on the second floor, that shy man whom they pointed to at a distance was Rawford. And Rawford was myself! And, thanks to me, thanks to the confidence which I inspired under the name of Rawford, the banks granted loans and the solicitors persuaded their clients to lend their money! Ah, I learned a useful lesson there, I assure you!'

He stopped suddenly, caught me by the arm, and, in a tone of exasperation in which, nevertheless, it was easy to perceive a certain shade of mingled admiration and irony, he added this ineffable phrase:

'My dear chap, at this moment, Gervaise Imbert owes me fifteen hundred francs!'

This time I could not help laughing. It was really a splendid joke, and Arsène himself joined in my laughter.

'Yes, my dear fellow, fifteen hundred francs! Not only did I not receive a sou of my salary, but she borrowed fifteen hundred francs of me! The whole savings of my youth! And do you know what for? I'll give you a thousand guesses . . . For her charities! I mean what I say! For poor people whom she pretended to be relieving, unknown to Ludovic! And I fell into the trap! A good joke, isn't it? Arsène Lupin done out of fifteen hundred francs, and done by the good lady whom he was robbing of four millions in forged securities! And think of the contrivings, the efforts, the ingenious tricks to which I had to resort in order to achieve that magnificent result! It's the only time that I've been swindled in my life! But, by Jove, I was had that time, and finely and in good taste!'

The Black Pearl

A violent ring at the bell woke the concierge at No. 9, Avenue Hoche from her sleep. She pulled the cord, muttering:

'I thought they were all in. It's past three!'

Her husband growled:

'Perhaps it's for the doctor.'

And a voice did, in fact, ask:

'Doctor Harel . . . which floor?'

'Third floor, on the left. But the doctor won't go out at night.'

'He'll have to, this time.'

The caller entered the hall, went up one floor, two floors, and, without even stopping on Dr. Harel's landing, continued as far as the fifth. Here he tried two keys; one opened the lock, the other unfastened the safety-catch.

'Capital,' he muttered. 'This simplifies matters considerably. But before setting to work let's provide for our retreat. Let me see . . . have I allowed a reasonable time for ringing at the doctor's and being dismissed by him? Not yet . . . I must wait a little longer.'

He let ten minutes elapse, then went

downstairs again and tapped at the pane of the porter's box, raging and fuming against the doctor as he did so. The front door was opened for him, and he slammed it behind him. But the door did not shut, for the man had quickly applied a piece of iron to the staple to prevent the bolt from entering.

He returned without a sound, unobserved by the concierge and her husband. In case of alarm, his retreat was assured.

He calmly reascended the five flights. Entering the hall of the flat, by the light of a portable electric lamp, he put his hat and coat on one of the chairs, sat down on another, and drew a pair of thick felt slippers over his boots.

'So much for that!' he said. 'And an easy job too! I sometimes ask myself why everybody doesn't choose the comfortable profession of a burglar. Given a little skill and reflective power, there's nothing more charming. It's such a restful trade, a regular family man's trade ... It's even too simple ... It ceases to be amusing ...'

He unfolded a minute plan of the flat.

'Let us begin by taking our bearings. Ah, here is the square hall in which I am sitting. Looking out on the street, we have the drawing-room, the boudoir, and the dining-room. No use wasting time there: it appears

233

the countess has very poor taste . . . there's not a knick-knack of the smallest value . . . So let's come to the point at once . . . Ah, here is a passage — the passage that leads to the bedrooms. At a distance of three yards I ought to find the door of the wardrobe-closet communicating with the countess's bedroom.'

He folded up his plan, put out his lantern, and walked down the passage, counting:

'One yard . . . two yards . . . three yards . . . Here is the door . . . How well it all fits in! Bless my soul! A mere bolt, a tiny bolt, separates me from the bedroom, and, moreover, I know that the bolt is three feet and a half from the floor . . . So that, with the aid of a little incision which I propose to make around it, we can easily get rid of it . . .'

He took the necessary implements from his pocket. But an idea stopped him.

'Supposing the bolt should happen to be unfastened . . . I may as well try.'

He turned the handle of the lock. To his great surprise the door opened.

'Arsène Lupin, my fine fellow, fortune's on your side to-night, there's no doubt of that! What do you want next? You know the geography of your field of operations; you know where the countess keeps the black pearl hidden . . . Consequently, the black pearl is yours . . . All that you have to do is to be more silent than silence itself, more invisible than the darkness.'

Arsène Lupin took quite half an hour to open the second door — a glass door leading to the bedroom. But he opened it with such infinite precautions that, even if the countess had been awake, no suspicious sound could have occurred to alarm her.

According to the indications marked on his plan, he had only to follow the circuit of a sofa. This would bring him first to an easy-chair, and then to a little table beside the bed. On the table was a box of stationery, and hidden quite simply inside this box was the black pearl.

He crouched at full length on the carpet, and followed the line of the sofa. But on reaching the end of it he stopped to check the beating of his heart. Although he felt no fear, he found it impossible to overcome that sort of nervous anguish which a man experiences in a silence that is greater than usual. And he was astonished at this, for, after all, he had passed through moments more solemn than the present without undergoing any sort of emotion. He was threatened by no danger. Then why was his heart beating like a mad bull? Was it that sleeping woman that impressed him, that life so close to his own?

He listened, and seemed to distinguish a rhythmical breathing. He felt reassured, as though by a friendly presence.

He found his way to the chair, and then, with little, imperceptible movements, crept towards the table, groping in the darkness with his out-stretched arm. His right hand touched one of the legs of the table.

At last! He had only to rise to his feet, take the black pearl, and go. It was as well, for his heart was again beginning to thump in his chest like a terrified animal, and so noisily that it seemed impossible that the countess should not wake.

He quieted it with a violent effort of will; but just as he was trying to rise his left hand struck against an object lying on the carpet, which he at once recognized as a candlestick — an overturned candlestick; and at the same moment another object offered to his touch: a clock — one of those little travelling-clocks in a leather case.

What did it all mean? What had happened? He could not understand. The clock . . . the candlestick . . . Why were they not in their usual places? Oh, what was happening in the frightful darkness?

And suddenly a cry escaped him. He had touched . . . oh, such a strange, unutterable thing! But no, no, fear must be affecting his brain! For twenty seconds, for thirty seconds, he lay motionless, terror-struck, with his temples bathed in perspiration. And his fingers retained the sensation of that touch.

With a relentless effort he put out his arm again. His hand once more grasped the thing — the strange, nameless thing. He felt it. He insisted that his hand should feel it and take stock of it . . . It was a head of hair, a face . . . and the face was cold — almost icy cold.

However terrifying a reality may be, a man like Arsène Lupin masters it as soon as he is aware of it. Quickly he pressed the spring of his lamp. A woman lay before him covered with blood. Her neck and shoulders were disfigured by hideous wounds. He stooped over her and examined her. She was dead.

'Dead! Dead!' he repeated, in his bewilderment.

And he looked at those staring eyes, that grinning mouth, that livid flesh, and that blood — all that blood, which had flowed upon the carpet, and was now congealing, thick and black.

He rose and switched on the electric light. He now saw that the room was filled with signs of a desperate struggle. The bed was entirely disordered, the sheets and blankets torn away. On the floor lay the candlestick, the clock (the hands pointed to twenty minutes past eleven), and, farther off, an overturned chair; and blood on every side — blood in pools and splashes.

'And the black pearl?' he muttered.

The box of stationary was in its place. He opened it hurriedly. It contained the jewel-case. But the case was empty.

'The devil!' he said. 'You boasted of your luck a bit too soon, my friend Arsène Lupin . . . The countess murdered, the black pearl gone . . . be off, or you will have a heavy responsibility on your shoulders!'

Nevertheless, he did not stir.

'Be off? Yes, another would be off. But Arsène Lupin? Is there nothing better to be done? Come, let us proceed by order. After all, your conscience is easy . . . Suppose that you were a police commissary, and had to make an inquiry? . . . Yes, but for that we should need a clearer brain. And mine is in such a state!'

He fell into a chair, pressing his clenched fists against his burning forehead.

★ ★ ★

The murder in the Avenue Hoche is one of the most puzzling of recent years, and I should never have been able to tell the story if the part played in it by Arsène Lupin had not thrown a special light upon it. There are few who suspect the nature of this part. In any case, no one knows the exact and curious facts.

Who, from seeing her driving in the Bois, did not know Léonide Zalti, the once famous opera-singer, who became the wife and widow of the Comte d'Andillot; the Zalti, whose luxurious mode of life dazzled Paris some twenty years ago; the Zalti, Comtesse d'Andillot, who owed an European reputation to the magnificence of her sets of diamonds and pearls? People used to say that she carried on her shoulders the strong-rooms of many a banking-house and the gold-mines of many an Australian company. The great jewellers worked for her much as they used to work for the kings and queens in the old days.

And who does not remember the catastrophe in which all these treasures were swallowed up? Banking-houses and gold-mines, the whirlpool devoured them all. Of the unparalleled collection, dispersed, amid great excitement, under the auctioneer's hammer, the countess retained only the famous black pearl. The black pearl — in other words, a fortune, had she been willing to part with it.

But she consistently refused. Rather than sell this priceless gem she preferred to economize, to live in a simple flat, just a companion, a cook, and a man-servant. Nor did she hesitate to confess her reason: the black pearl was the gift of an emperor! And though almost ruined and reduced to the most ordinary sort of existence, she remained faithful to the companion of her better days.

'As long as I live,' she said, 'it shall never quit my sight.'

She wore it round her neck from morning till evening. At night she placed in a receptacle known to herself alone.

All these facts were related in the newspapers, and stimulated public curiosity. And, strange to say, though easy enough to understand for those who possess the key to the riddle, it was just the arrest of the alleged assassin that complicated the mystery and increased the excitement. Two days after the murder the papers contained the following news:

We understand that Victor Danègre, the Comtesse d'Andillot's servant, has been arrested. The evidence adduced against him is overwhelming. Bloodstains have been discovered on the lustrine sleeve of his livery waistcoat, which was found in his room, hidden between the mattresses of his bed, by M. Dudouis, the chief of the detective service. Moreover, one of the stuff-covered buttons of the waistcoat was missing; and this button had been picked up, at an early stage of the investigation, under the victim's bed.

It seems probable that, after dinner, instead of going to his own room in the attic, Danègre slipped into the wardrobe-closet, and through the glass door saw the countess hide the black pearl.

We must add that there is no proof, so far, to confirm this supposition. In any case, one point remains unexplained. At seven o'clock in the morning Danègre went to the tobacconist's shop on the Boulevard de Courcelles. The concierge and the tobacconist have both given evidence to this effect. On the other hand, the countess's cook and her companion, both of whom sleep at the end of the passage, declare that at eight o'clock, when they got up, the front door and the kitchen door were double-locked. The two women have been in the countess's service for over twenty years, *and are above suspicion. The question is, How was Danègre able to leave the flat? Did he have another key made for his own use? The inquiry will show.*

The inquiry showed absolutely nothing. On the contrary. It appeared that Victor Danègre was a dangerous criminal, who had already served a term of imprisonment, a confirmed drunkard and loose-liver, who was not likely to quail before the use of the knife. But the case itself seemed to become wrapped in a thicker shroud of mystery and in more inexplicable contradictions the more it was studied.

To begin with, Mlle. de Sinclèves, the cousin and sole heiress of the murdered woman, declared that the countess, a month before her death, told her, in one of her letters, of the place where she used to hide the black pearl. This letter disappeared the day after she received it. Who had stolen it?

The concierge and his wife, on their side, said that they had opened the door to a man who had gone up to Dr. Harel's. The doctor was sent for. No one had rung at his door. In that case, who was this man? An accomplice?

This idea of an accomplice was adopted by the newspapers and the public. Ganimard — old Chief-Inspector Ganimard — accepted it, not without excuse.

'Lupin has had a hand in this,' he said to the examining magistrate.

'Bah! You see that Arsène Lupin of yours in everything.'

'I see him in everything, because he is in everything.'

'Say rather that you see him whenever anything does not seem very clear to you. Besides, in this particular case, remember that the crime was committed at twenty minutes past eleven in the evening, as the clock shows, and that the night visit described by the concierge and his wife did not take place until three o'clock in the morning.'

The police often yield to a sort of conviction that makes them force events so as to fit in with the first explanation offered. Victor Danègre's antecedents were of a deplorable character — I have already said that he had undergone sentence before, was a drunkard and a loose-liver — and this influenced magistrate's judgment. Although no new circumstance arose to corroborate the first two or three clues, he refused to be shaken. He closed the inquiry, and a few weeks later the trial began.

It dragged wearily along. The presiding judge took no interest in the case. The prosecution was feebly conducted. Under these conditions, Danègre's counsel had an easy game to play. He pointed to the gaps and impossibilities in the evidence. There was no material proof in existence. Who had made the key, the indispensable key, without which Danègre could not have double-locked the door of the flat on leaving? Who had seen this key, and what had become of it? Who had seen the murderer's knife, and what had become of that?

'In any case,' said the counsel, in conclusion, 'it rests with the prosecution to prove that my client committed the murder. Let them prove that the perpetrator of the theft and the murder is not the mysterious individual who entered the house at three o'clock in the morning. The clock stopped at eleven at night, they say. And then? Cannot the hands of a clock be shifted to any hour that seems convenient?'

Victor Danègre was acquitted.

★ ★ ★

He left prison one Friday by the waning light of the afternoon, emaciated and depressed by the six months spent in the cells. The examination, the solitary confinement, the trial, the deliberation of the jury — all this had filled him with a sickly dread. His nights were haunted by hideous nightmares and visions of the scaffold. He trembled with fever and terror.

Under the name of Anatole Dufour he hired a small room on the heights of Montmartre, and lived on odd jobs — shifting for himself as best he could.

A wretched life! Thrice engaged by three different employers, he was each time recognized as Victor Danègre, and dismissed on the spot.

He often saw, or thought he saw, men following him — men, he had no doubt, belonging to the police, who would never rest until they had caught him in some trap. Already he felt a rough hand seize him by the collar.

One evening he was dining at an eating-house in the neighbourhood when some one came and sat down opposite him. It was a man of about forty years of age, dressed in a black frock-coat of doubtful cleanliness. He ordered a soup, a dish of vegetables, and a quart of wine. And when he had eaten his soup he looked at Danègre with a long fixed stare.

Danègre turned pale. Without a doubt the man was one of those who had been following him for weeks. What did he want with him? Danègre tried to get up. He could not. His legs staggered beneath him.

The stranger poured himself out a glass of wine, and filled Danègre's glass.

'Have a drink, mate?'

Victor stammered:

'Thanks . . . thanks . . . your health, mate.'

'Your health, Victor Danègre.'

The other gave a start.

'I! I! . . . No . . . I assure you . . . '

'You assure me what? That you are not yourself? Not the servant of the countess?'

'Whose servant? My name is Dufour. Ask the landlord.'

'Anatole Dufour, yes, to the landlord, but Danègre, Victor Danègre, to the police.'

'It's not true, it's not true! They've told you a lie.'

The newcomer took a card from his pocket and handed it to him. Victor read:

GRIMAUDAN
Ex-Detective-Inspector
Confidential Inquiries

He shivered.

'You belong to the police!'

'Not now; but I used to like the trade, and I still follow it . . . in a more lucrative way. From time to time one lights upon a golden job . . . like yours.'

'Mine?'

'Yes, yours is an exceptional case — at least, if you care to show a little willingness in the matter.'

'And if I don't?'

'You'll have to. You're in a position in which you can refuse me nothing.'

Victor Danègre felt himself overcome by a dull sense of fear. He asked:

'What is it? . . . Speak out!'

'Very well,' said the other, let's come to the point and have done with it. In two words, I have been sent by Mademoiselle de Sinclèves.'

'Sinclèves?'

'The Comtesse d'Andillot's heiress.'

'Well?'

'Well, Mademoiselle de Sinclèves has employed me in order to make you give up the black pearl.'

'The black pearl?'

'The one you stole.'

'But I haven't got it.'

'Yes, you have.'

'If I had, I should be the murderer.'

'You are the murderer.'

Danègre gave a forced laugh.

'Fortunately, my good sir, the court took another view. The jury unanimously found me not guilty. And when a man has conscience on his side, together with the esteem of twelve good men and true . . . '

The ex-detective-inspector seized him by the arm.

'None of your speech-making, my lad. Listen to me carefully, and weigh my words: they are worth it. Three months before the crime, Danègre, you stole the key of the servants' entrance from the cook and you had a similar one made at Outard's, the locksmith, 244, Rue Oberkampf.'

'It's not true! it's not true!' growled Victor. 'No one has seen the key; there's no such key.'

'Here it is!'

After a silence, Grimaudan resumed:

'You killed the countess with a clasp-knife which you bought at the Bazar de la République on the same day that you ordered the key. It has a three-cornered, grooved blade.'

'All humbug! You're talking at random. No one has seen the knife.'

'Here it is!'

Victor Danègre started back. The ex-inspector continued:

'There are stains of rust on the blade. Do you want me to explain to you where they come from?'

'And then? . . . You've got a key and a knife

. . . Who can swear that they belong to me?'

'The locksmith first, and next the shop-assistant from whom you bought the knife. I have already refreshed their memories. Once brought face to face with you, they would not fail to recognize you.'

He spoke shortly and sharply, with terrifying precision. Danègre was convulsed with fear. Neither the magistrate nor the judge at his trial, nor even the prosecution counsel, had pressed him so closely — had seen so clearly into matters which were no longer even very plain to him.

However, he still tried to make a show of indifference.

'If that's all your evidence!'

'I have this besides. After the crime you went back by the way you came. But half-way across the wardrobe-closet, seized with fright, you must have leaned against the wall to keep your balance.'

'How do you know?' stammered Victor . . . 'No one can know.'

'The police, no; it could never have entered the heads of any of the gentlemen in the office of the public prosecutor to light a candle and examine the walls. But if they were to do so they would see a red mark on the white plaster, a very slight mark, but clear enough to show the impression of your thumb, all wet with blood, which you put against the wall. Now you are surely aware that, in the Bertillon system, this forms one of the chief methods of identification.'

Victor Danègre was deathly pale. Beads of perspiration fell from his forehead to the table. He stared mad-eyed at this strange man who was conjuring up his crime as though he had been its unseen witness.

He lowered his head, beaten, powerless. For months he had been struggling — struggling, as it seemed to him, against the whole world. Against this man he had the impression that there was nothing to be done.

'If I give you back the pearl,' he stuttered, 'how much will you give me?'

'Nothing.'

'What! You're joking! You expect me to give you a thing worth thousands and hundreds of thousands of francs and you to give me nothing?'

'Yes, your life.'

The wretched man shuddered. Grimaudan added, in an almost gentle tone:

'Come, Danègre, the pearl is of no value to you. You cannot possibly sell it. What is the good of keeping it?'

'There are receivers . . . and some day or other, at a price . . . '

'Some day or other will be too late.'

'Why?'

'Why? Because the police will have laid you by the heels again, and this time, with the proofs with which I shall supply them — the knife, the key, the thumb-print — you're done for, my fine fellow.'

Victor clutched his head in his two hands and reflected. He felt himself lost, irreparably lost, and, at the same time, a great sense of weariness overcame him, an immense need of rest and ease.

He muttered:

'When do you want it?'

'Before one o'clock tonight'

'And if you don't get it?'

'If I don't get it I shall post this letter, in which Mademoiselle de Sinclèves denounces you to the public prosecutor.'

Danègre poured himself out two glasses of wine, swallowed them one after the other, and then, rising:

'Pay the bill,' he said, 'and let's go . . . I've had enough of this cursed business.'

★   ★   ★

Night had come. The two men went down the Rue Lepic, and along the outer boulevards towards the Étoile. They walked in silence, Victor very wearily, with a bent back.

At the Parc Monceau he said:

'It's close by the house . . . '

'By Jove, you only left it, before your arrest, to go to the tobacco-shop!'

'We're there,' said Danègre, in a hollow voice.

They went along the railings of the garden, and crossed a street of which the corner was formed by the tobacconist's shop. Danègre stopped a few paces farther on. His legs reeled under him. He dropped on a bench.

'Well?' asked his companion.

'It's there.'

'It's there? What are you talking about?'

'Yes, there, in front of us.'

'In front of us? Look here, Danègre, you had better not . . . '

'I tell you, it's there.'

'Where?'

'Between two paving-stones.'

'Which two?'

'Find it yourself.'

'Which two?' repeated Grimaudan.

Victor did not reply.

'Ah, I see, you're trying to hoodwink me, are you?'

'No . . . but . . . I shall die of starvation . . . '

'And so you're hesitating? Well, I'll be generous with you. How much do you want?'

'Enough to pay my passage to America.'

'Agreed.'

'And a hundred-franc note for expenses.'

'You shall have two. And now speak.'

'Count the cobbles to the right of the drain. It's between the twelfth and the thirteenth.'

'In the gutter?'

'Yes, just below the curb-stone.'

Grimaudan looked around him. Tram-cars were passing, people were passing on foot. But, pooh! Who would suspect? . . .

He opened his pocket-knife, and thrust it between the twelfth and thirteenth cobble-stones.

'And if it's not there?'

'If no one saw me stoop and push it in, it must be there still.'

Could it be there? The black pearl flung into the mud of a gutter for the first passer-by to pick up! The black pearl . . . a fortune!

'How far down?'

'About three inches.'

He made an opening in the moist earth. The point of his knife struck against something. He widened the hole with his fingers.

The black pearl was there.

'Here, take your two hundred francs. I'll send you your ticket for America.'

The next evening the *Écho de France* published the following paragraph, which was copied by the press of the whole world:

Yesterday the famous black pearl fell into the hands of Arsène Lupin, who recovered it from the murderer of the Comtesse d'Andillot. Facsimilies of this valuable jewel will shortly be exhibited in London, St. Petersburg, Calcutta, Buenos Ayres, and New York.

Arsène Lupin is prepared to receive offers from his correspondents at home and abroad.'

'And that is how crime is always punished and virtue rewarded,' concluded Arsène Lupin, after he had revealed to me the unknown side of the story.

'I see; that is how, under the name of Grimaudan, an ex-detective-inspector, you were selected by fate to deprive the criminal of the fruits of his crime!'

'Exactly. And I confess that it is one of the adventures of which I am most proud. The forty minutes which I spent in the countess's flat, after verifying her death, I number among the most astonishing and the most

254

momentous in my life. Caught in an apparently inextricable situation, in forty minutes I had reconstructed the crime, and, thanks to a few signs, acquired by the certainty that the murderer could be none other than one of the countess's servants. Lastly, I saw that, if I was to have the pearl, the man must be arrested, and so I left the waistcoat-button. But that there must not be any irrefutable proofs of his guilt, I picked up the knife which he had left on the carpet, took away the key which he had left in the lock, double-locked the door and removed the finger-marks on the plaster of the wardrobe-closet. In my opinion, this was one of those flashes . . . '

'Of genius,' I put in.

'Of genius, if you like, which would not have lit up the brain of the first-comer. I hit, in one second, upon the two terms of the problem — an arrest and and acquittal — and made use of the formidable apparatus of the law to unsettle my man, to stupefy him, and, in short, to reduce him to such a condition of mind that, once free, he must inevitably, fatally fall into the rather clumsy trap which I had laid for him.'

'Rather clumsy? I should say very! For he ran no danger.'

'No, none at all, for a man can't be tried

twice for the same offence.'

'Poor devil! . . . '

'Poor devil! . . . Victor Danègre? You forget that he's a murderer! . . . It would have been a most immoral thing to leave the black pearl in his possession. Why, he's alive! Just think, Danègre's alive!'

'And the black pearl is yours.'

He took it from one of the secret compartments of his pocket-book, examined it with loving fingers and earnest eyes, and sighed.

'What Russian prince, what vain and idiot Rajah, will end by becoming the owner of this treasure? What American millionaire is destined to possess this morsel of beauty and luxury which once adorned the white shoulders of Léonide Zalti, Comtesse d'Andillot? Who can tell? . . . '

Sherlock Holmes Arrives Too Late

'It's really curious, your likeness to Arsène Lupin, my dear Velmont.'

'Do you know him?'

'Oh, just as everybody does — by his photographs, not one of which in the least resembles the others; but they all leave the impression of the same face . . . which is undoubtedly yours.'

Horace Velmont seemed rather annoyed.

'I suppose you're right Devanne. You're not the first to tell me of it, I assure you.'

'Upon my word,' persisted Devanne, 'if you had not been introduced to me by my cousin d'Estavan, and if you were not the well-known painter whose charming sea-pieces I admire so much, I'm not sure but that I should have informed the police of your presence at Dieppe.'

The sally was received with general laughter. There were gathered, in the great dining-room of Thibermesnil Castle, in addition to Velmont, the Abbé Gélis, rector of the village, and a dozen officers whose

257

regiments were taking part in the manoeuvres in the neighbourhood, and who had accepted the invitation of Georges Devanne, the banker, and his mother. One of them exclaimed:

'But, I say, wasn't Arsène Lupin seen on the coast after his famous performance in the train between Paris and Le Havre?'

'Just so, three months ago; and the week after I made the acquaintance, at the Casino, of our friend Velmont here, who has since honoured me with a few visits: an agreeable preliminary to a more serious call which I presume he means to pay me one of these days . . . or, rather, one of these nights!'

The company laughed once more, and moved into the old guard-room — a huge, lofty hall which occupies the whole of the lower portion of the Tower Guillaume, and which Georges Devanne has arranged all the incomparable treasures accumulated through the centuries by the lords of Thibermesnil. It is filled and adorned with old chests and credence-tables, fire-dogs and candelabra. Splendid tapestries hang on the stone walls. The deep embrasures of the four windows are furnished with seats and end in pointed casements with leaded panes. Between the door and the window on the left stands a monumental Renaissance book-case, on the pediment of which is inscribed, in gold letters, the word

THIBERMESNIL

and underneath it is the proud motto of the family:

Fais ce que veux
(Do what thou wilt)

And as they were lighting their cigars, Devanne added:

'But you will have to hurry, Velmont, for this is the last night on which you will have a chance.'

'And why the last night?' said the painter, who certainly took the jest in very good part.

Devanne was about to reply when his mother made signs to him. But the excitement of the dinner and the wish to interest his guests were too much for him:

'Pooh!' he muttered. 'Why shouldn't I tell them? There's no indiscretion to be feared now.'

They sat round him, filled with a lively curiosity, and he declared, with the self-satisfied air of a man announcing a great piece of news:

'To-morrow, at four o'clock in the afternoon, I shall have here, as my guest, Sherlock Holmes, the great English detective, for whom no mystery exists, the most extraordinary solver of riddles that has ever been known, the wonderful individual who might have been the creation of a novelist's brain.'

There was a general exclamation. Sherlock Holmes at Thibermesnil! The thing was serious, then? Was Arsène Lupin really in the district?

'Arsène Lupin and his gang are not very far away. Without counting Baron Cahorn's mishap, to whom are we to ascribe the daring burglaries at Montigny and Gruchet and Crasville if not to our national thief? To-day it's my turn.'

'And have you had a warning, like Baron Cahorn?'

'The same trick does not succeed twice.'

'Then? . . . '

'Look here.'

He rose, and, pointing to a little empty space between two tall folios on one of the shelves of the bookcase, said:

'There was a book here — a sixteenth-century book, entitled *The Chronicles of Thibermesnil* — which was the history of the castle since the time of its construction by Duke Rollo, on the site of a feudal fortress. It contained three engraved plates. One of them presented a general view of the domain as a whole; the second a plan of the building; and the third — I call your special attention to this — the sketch of an underground passage, one of whose outlets opens outside the first line of the ramparts, while the other ends here — yes, in this very hall where we are sitting. Now this book disappeared last month.'

'By Jove!' said Velmont, 'that's a bad sign. Only it's not enough to justify the intervention of Sherlock Holmes.'

'Certainly it would not have been enough if another fact had not come to give its full significance to that which I have just told you. There is a second copy of the chronicle in the Bibliothèque Nationale, and the two copies differed in certain details concerning the underground passage, such as the addition of a sectional drawing, and a scale and a number of notes, not printed, but written in ink and more or less obliterated. I knew of these particulars, and I knew that the definite sketch could not be reconstructed except by carefully comparing the two plans. Well, on the day after that on which my copy disappeared the one in the Bibliothèque Nationale was applied for by a reader who carried it off without any clue as to the manner in which the theft had been effected.'

These words were greeted with many exclamations.

'This time the affair grows serious.'

'Yes; and this time,' said Devanne, 'the police were roused, and there was a double inquiry which, however, led to no result.

'Like all those aimed at Arsène Lupin.'

'Exactly. It then occurred to me to write and ask for the help of Sherlock Holmes, who replied that he had the keenest wish to come into contact with Arsène Lupin.'

'What an honour for Arsène Lupin!' said Velmont. 'But if our national thief, as you call him, should not be contemplating a project upon Thibermesnil, then there will be nothing for Sherlock Holmes to do but twiddle his thumbs.'

'There is another matter which is sure to interest him: the discovery of the underground passage.'

'Why, you told us that one end opened in the fields and the other here, in the guardroom!'

'Yes, but in what part of it?' The line that represents the tunnel on the plans finishes, at one end, at a little circle accompanied by the initials T. G., which, of course, stands for Tower Guillaume. But it's a round tower, and who can decide at which point in the circle the line in the drawing touches?'

Devanne lit a second cigar, and poured himself out a glass of Benedictine. The others pressed him with questions. He smiled with pleasure at the interest which he had aroused. At last, he said:

'The secret is lost. Not a person in the world knows it. The story says that the high and mighty lords handed it down to one another, on their death-beds, from father to son, until the day when Geoffrey, the last of the name, lost his head on the scaffold, on the seventh of Thermidor, Year Second, in the nineteenth year of his age.'

'Yes, but more than a century has passed since then; and it must have been looked for.'

'It has been looked for, but in vain. I myself, after I bought the castle from the great-grand-nephew of Leribourg of the National Convention, had excavations made. What was the good? Remember that this tower is surrounded by water on every side, and only joined to the castle by a bridge, and that, consequently, the tunnel must pass under the old moats. The plan in the Bibliothèque Nationale shows a series of four staircases, comprising forty-eight steps, which allows for a depth of over ten yards, and the scale·annexed to the other plans fixes the length at two hundred yards. As a matter of fact, the whole problem lies here, between this floor, that ceiling, and these walls; and, upon my word, I do not feel inclined to have them pulled down.'

'And is there no clue?'

'Not one.'

The Abbé Gélis objected.

'Monsieur Devanne, we have to reckon with two quotations . . . '

'Oh,' cried Devanne, laughing, 'the rector is a great rummager of family papers, a great reader of memoirs, and he fondly loves everything that has to do with Thibermesnil. But the explanation to which he refers only serves to confuse matters.'

'But tell us what it is.'

'Do you really care to hear?'

'Immensely.'

'Well, you must know that, as a result of his reading, he has discovered that two kings of France held the key to the riddle.'

'Two kings of France?'

'Henry IV and Louis the XVI.'

'Two famous men. And how did the rector find out?'

'Oh, it's very simple,' continued Devanne. 'Two days before the battle of Arques, King Henry IV came to sup and sleep in the castle. At eleven o'clock, Louise de Tonquerville, the prettiest lady in Normandy, was brought into the castle through the subterranian passage by Duke Edgar, who at the same time confided the secret to the King. This secret Henry IV revealed later to Sully, his minister, who tells the story in his *Royales Economies d'État*, without adding any comment besides this incomprehensible phrase: 'Turn one eye on the bee that shakes, the other eye will lead to God.'

A silence followed, and Velmont laughed:

'It's not as clear as daylight, is it?'

'That's what I say. The rector maintains that Sully set down the key to the puzzle by means of those words, without betraying the secret to the scribes to whom he dictated his memoirs.'

'It's an ingenious supposition.'

'True. But what is the eye that turns? What is the bee that shakes?'

'And who goes to God?'

'Goodness knows!'

'And what about our good King Louis XVI.? Was it also to receive a lady that he caused the passage to be opened?' asked Velmont.

'I don't know,' said M. Devanne. 'All I can say is Louis XVI. stayed at Thibermesnil in 1784, and the famous Iron Cupboard discovered at the Louvre on the information of the Gamain, the locksmith, contained a paper with these words written in the king's hand: 'Thibermesnil, 3–4–11.'' (4)

Horace Velmont laughed aloud.

'Victory! The darkness is dispelled!'

'Laugh as you please, sir,' said the rector. 'Those two quotations contain the solution for all that, and one of these days some one will come along who knows how to interpret them.'

'Sherlock Holmes is the man,' said Devanne, 'unless Arsène Lupin forestalls him. What do you think, Velmont?'

Velmont rose, laid his hand on Devanne's shoulder, and declared:

'I think that the data supplied by your book and the copy in the Bibliothèque Nationale lacked just one link of the highest importance, and that you have been kind enough to supply it. I am much obliged to you.'

'Well? . . . '

'Well, now that the eye has turned and the bee has shaken, all I have to do is set to work.'

'Without losing a minute?'

'Without losing a second! You see, I must rob your castle to-night, that is to say, before Sherlock Holmes arrives.'

'You're quite right; you have only just got time. Would you like me to drive you?'

'To Dieppe?'

'Yes, I may as well fetch Monsieur and

266

Madame d'Androl and a young lady friend of theirs, who are arriving by the midnight train.'

Then, turning to the officers:

'We shall all meet here at lunch to-morrow, shan't we, gentlemen? I rely upon you, for the castle is to be invested by your regiments and taken by assault at eleven in the morning.'

The invitation was accepted, the officers took their leave, and a minute later a powerful motorcar was carrying Devanne and Velmont along the Dieppe road. Devanne dropped the painter at the Casino, and went on to the station.

His friends arrived at midnight, and at half-past twelve the motor passed through the gates of Thibermesnil. At one o'clock, after a light supper served in the drawing-room, every one went to bed. The lights were extinguished one by one. The deep silence of the night enshrouded the castle.

★　★　★

But the moon pierced the clouds that veiled it, and, through two of the windows, filled the hall with the light of its white beams. This lasted for but a moment. Soon the moon was hidden behind the curtain of the hills, and all was darkness. The silence increased as the shadows thickened. At most it was disturbed, from time to time, by the creaking of the furniture or the rustling of the reeds in the pond which bathes the old walls with its green waters.

The clock told the endless ticks of its seconds. It struck two. Then once more the seconds fell hastily and monotonously in the heavy stillness of the night. Then three struck. And suddenly something gave a clash, like the arm of a railway-signal that drops as a train passes, and a thin streak of light crossed the hall from one end to the other, like an arrow, leaving a glittering track behind it. It issued from the central groove of a pilaster against which the pediment of the bookcase rests upon the right. It lingered upon the opposite panel in a dazzling circle, next wandered on every side like a restless glance searching the darkness, and then faded away, only to appear once more, while the whole of one section of the bookcase turned upon its axis, and revealed a wide opening shaped like a vault.

A man entered, holding an electric lantern in his hand. Another man and a third emerged, carrying a coil of rope and different implements. The first man looked round the room, listened, and said:

'Call the others.'

Eight men came out of the underground

passage — eight strapping fellows, with determined faces. And the removal began.

It did not take long. Arsène Lupin passed from one piece to another, examined it, and, according to its size or its artistic value, spared it or gave an order:

'Take it away.'

And the piece in question was removed, swallowed by the yawning mouth of the tunnel, and sent down into the bowels of the earth.

And thus were juggled away six Louis XV. armchairs and as many occasional chairs, a number of Aubusson tapestries, some candelabra signed by Gouthière, two Fragonards and a Nattier, a bust by Houdon, and some statuettes. At times Arsène Lupin would stop before a magnificent oak chest or a splendid picture and sigh:

'That's too heavy . . . Too big . . . What a pity!'

And he would continue his expert survey.

In forty minutes the hall was 'cleared,' to use Arsène's expression. And all this was accomplished in an admirably orderly manner, without the least noise, as though all the objects which the men were handling had been wrapped in thick wadding.

To the last man who was leaving, carrying a clock signed by Boule, he said:

'You need not come back. You understand, don't you, that as soon as the motor-van is loaded you're to make for the barn at Roquefort?'

'What about yourself, governor?'

'Leave me the motor-cycle.'

When the man had gone he pushed the movable section of the bookcase back into its place, and, after clearing away the traces of the removal and the footmarks, he raised a curtain and entered a gallery which served as a communication between the tower and the castle. Half-way down the gallery stood a glass case, and it was because of this case that Arsène Lupin had continued his investigations.

It contained marvels: an unique collection of watches, snuff-boxes, rings, chatelaines, miniatures of the most exquisite workmanship. He forced the lock with a jimmy, and it was an unspeakable pleasure to him to finger those gems of gold and silver, those precious and dainty little works of art.

Hanging round his neck was a large canvas bag specially contrived to hold these windfalls. He filled it. He also filled the pockets of his jacket, waistcoat, and trousers. And he was stuffing under his left arm a heap of those pearl reticules beloved of our ancestors and so eagerly sought after by our present fashion . . . when a slight sound fell upon his ear.

He listened; he was not mistaken; the noise became clearer.

And suddenly he remembered. At the end of the gallery an inner staircase led to a room which had been hitherto unoccupied, but which had been allotted that evening to the young girl whom Devanne had gone to meet at Dieppe with his friends the d'Androls.

With a quick movement he pressed the spring of his lantern and extinguished it. He had just time to hide in the recess of a window when the door at the top of the staircase opened and the gallery was lit by a faint gleam.

He had a feeling — for, half-hidden behind a curtain, he could not see — that a figure was cautiously descending the top stairs. He hoped that it would come no farther. It continued, however, and took several steps into the gallery. But it gave a cry. It must have caught sight of the broken case, three-quarters emptied of its contents.

By the scent he recognized the presence of a woman. Her dress almost touched the curtain that concealed him, and he seemed to hear her heart beating, while she must needs herself perceive the presence of another person behind her in the dark, within reach of her hand. He said to himself:

'She's frightened . . . she'll go back . . . she is bound to go back.'

She did not go back. The candle shaking in her hand became steadier. She turned round, hesitated for a moment, appeared to be listening to the alarming silence, and then, with a sudden movement, pulled back the curtain.

Their eyes met.

Arsène murmured, in confusion:

'You . . . you . . . Miss Nellie!'

It was Nellie Underdown, the passenger on the Provence, the girl who had mingled her dreams with his during that never-to-be-forgotten crossing, who had witnessed his arrest, and who, rather than betray him, had generously flung into the sea the Kodak in which he had hidden the stolen jewels and bank-notes! . . . It was Nellie Underdown, the dear, sweet girl whose image had so often saddened or gladdened his long hours spent in prison!

So extraordinary was their chance meeting in this castle and at that hour of the night that they did not stir, did not utter a word, dumfounded and, as it were, hypnotized by the fantastic apparition which each of them presented to the other's eyes.

Nellie, shattered with emotion, staggered to a seat.

He remained standing in front of her. And gradually, as the interminable seconds passed, he became aware of the impression which he must be making at that moment, with his arms loaded with curiosities, his pockets stuffed, his bag filled to bursting. A great sense of confusion mastered him, and he blushed to find himself there in the mean plight of a thief caught in the act. To her henceforth, come what may, he was the thief, the man who puts his hand into other men's pockets, the man who picks locks and enters doors by stealth.

One of the watches rolled upon the carpet, followed by another. And more things came slipping from under his arms, which were unable to retain them. Then, quickly making up his mind, he dropped a part of his booty into a chair, emptied his pockets, and took off his bag.

He now felt easier in Nellie's presence, and took a step towards her, with the intention of speaking to her. But she made a movement of recoil and rose quickly, as though seized with fright, and ran to the guard-room. The curtain fell behind her. He followed her. She stood there, trembling and speechless, and her eyes gazed in terror upon the great devastated hall.

Without a moment's hesitation, he said:

'At three o'clock tomorrow everything shall be restored to its place . . . The things shall be brought back.'

She did not reply; and he repeated:

'At three o'clock tomorrow, I give you my solemn pledge . . . No power on earth shall prevent me from keeping my promise . . . At three o'clock tomorrow.'

A long silence weighed upon them both. He dared not break it, and the girl's emotion made him suffer in every nerve. Softly, without a word, he moved away.

And he thought to himself:

'She must go! . . . She must feel that she is free to go! . . . She must not be afraid of me! . . . '

But suddenly she started, and stammered:

'Hark! . . . Footsteps! . . . I hear someone coming . . . '

He looked at her with surprise. She appeared distraught, as though at the approach of danger.

'I hear nothing,' he said, 'and even so . . . '

'Why, you must fly! . . . Quick, fly! . . . '

'Fly . . . why?'

'You must! . . . you must! . . . Ah, don't stay!'

She rushed to the entrance to the gallery

and listened. No, there was no one there. Perhaps the sound had come from the outside ... She waited a second, and then, reassured, turned round.

Arsène Lupin had disappeared.

★ ★ ★

Devanne's first thought, on ascertaining that his castle had been pillaged, found expression in the words which he spoke to himself:

'This is Velmont's work, and Velmont is none other than Arsène Lupin.'

All was explained by this means, and nothing could be explained by any other. And yet the idea only just passed through his mind, for it seemed almost impossible that Velmont should not be Velmont — that is to say, the well-known painter, the club friend of his cousin d'Estavan. And when the sergeant of gendarmes had been sent for and arrived, Devanne did not even think of telling him of this absurd conjecture.

The whole of that morning was spent, at Thibermesnil, in an indescribable hubbub. The gendarmes, the rural police, the commissary of police from Dieppe, the inhabitants of the village thronged the passages, the park, the approaches to the castle. The arrival of the troops taking part in the manoeuvres and the crack of the rifles added to the picturesqueness of the scene.

The early investigations furnished no clue. The windows had not been broken nor the doors smashed in. There was no doubt but that the removal had been effected through the secret passage. And yet there was no trace of footsteps on the carpet, no unusual mark upon the walls.

There was one unexpected thing, however, which clearly pointed to the fanciful methods of Arsène Lupin: the famous sixteenth-century chronicle had been restored to its old place in the bookcase, and beside it stood a similar volume, which was none other than the copy stolen from the Bibliothèque Nationale.

The officers arrived at eleven. Devanne received them gaily; however annoyed he might feel at the loss of his artistic treasures, his fortune was large enough to enable him to bear it without showing ill-humour. His friends the d'Androls and Nellie came down from their rooms, and the officers were introduced.

One of the guests was missing: Horace Velmont. Was he not coming? He walked in upon the stroke of twelve, and Devanne exclaimed:

'Good! There you are at last!'

'Am I late?'

'No, but you might have been . . . after such an exciting night! You have heard the news, I suppose?'

'What news?'

'You robbed the castle last night.'

'Nonsense!'

'I tell you, you did. But give your arm to Miss Underdown, and let us go in to lunch . . . Miss Underdown, let me introduce . . . '

He stopped, struck by the confusion on the girl's features. Then, seized with a sudden recollection, he said:

'Ah, of course, you once travelled on the same ship with Arsène Lupin . . . before his arrest . . . You are surprised by the likeness, no doubt?'

She did not reply. Velmont stood before her, smiling. He bowed; she took his arm. He led her to her place, and sat down opposite to her . . .

During lunch they talked of nothing but Arsène Lupin, the stolen furniture, the underground passage, and Sherlock Holmes. Not until the end of the meal, when other subjects were broached, did Velmont join in the conversation. He was amusing and serious, eloquent and witty, by turns. And whatever he said he appeared to say with the sole object of interesting Nellie. She, wholly engrossed in her own thoughts, seemed not to hear him.

Coffee was served on the terrace overlooking the court-yard and the French garden in front of the castle. The regimental band played on the lawn, and a crowd of peasants and soldiers strolled about the walks in the park.

Nellie was thinking of Arsène Lupin's promise:

'At three o'clock everything will be returned. I give you my solemn pledge.'

At three o'clock! And the hands of the great clock in the right wing pointed to twenty to three. In spite of herself, she kept looking at it. And she also looked at Velmont, who was swinging peacefully in a comfortable rocking chair.

Ten minutes to three . . . five minutes to three . . . A sort of impatience, mingled with a sense of exquisite pain, racked the young girl's mind. Was it possible for the miracle to be accomplished and to be accomplished at the fixed time, when the castle, the court-yard, and the country around were filled with people, and when, at that very moment, the public prosecutor and the examining magistrate were pursuing their investigations?

And still . . . still, Arsène Lupin had given

such a solemn promise!

'It will happen just as he said,' she thought, impressed by all the man's energy, authority, and certainty.

And it seemed to her no longer a miracle, but a natural event that was bound to take place in the ordinary course of things.

For a second their eyes met. She blushed, and turned her head away.

Three o'clock . . . The first stroke rang out, the second, the third . . . Horace Velmont took out his watch, glanced up at the clock, and put his watch back in his pocket. A few seconds elapsed. And then the crowd opened out around the lawn to make way for two carriages that had just passed through the park gates, each drawn by two horses. They were two of those regimental wagons which carry the cooking-utensils of the officers' mess and the soldier's kits. They stopped in front of the steps. A quarter-master sergeant jumped down from the box of the first wagon and asked for M. Devanne.

Devanne ran down the steps. Under the awnings, carefully packed and wrapped up, were his pictures, his furniture, his works of art of all kinds.

The sergeant replied to the questions put to him by producing the order which the adjutant on duty had given him, and which the adjutant himself received that morning in the orderly room. The order stated that No. 2 company of the fourth battalion was to see that the goods and chattels deposited at the Halleux crossroads, in the Forest of Arques, were delivered at three o'clock to M. Georges Devanne, the owner of Thibermesnil Castle. It bore the signature of Colonel Beauvel.

'I found everything ready for us at the crossroads,' added the sergeant, 'laid out on the grass, under the charge of . . . any one passing. That struck me as queer, but . . . well, sir, the order was plain enough!'

One of the officers examined the signature: it was a good copy, but forged.

The band had stopped. The wagons were emptied, and the furniture carried indoors.

In the midst of this excitement Nellie Underdown was left standing alone at one end of the terrace. She was grave and anxious, full of vague thoughts, which she did not seek to formulate. Suddenly she saw Velmont coming up to her. She wished to avoid him, but the corner of the balustrade that borders the terrace hemmed her in on two sides, and a row of great tubs of shrubs — orange-trees, laurels, and bamboos — left her no other way of escape than that by which Velmont was approaching. She did not move. A ray of sunlight quivered on her golden hair, shaken by the frail leaves of a bamboo-plant. She heard a soft voice say:

'Have I not kept my promise I made you last night?'

Arsène Lupin stood by her side, and there was no one else near them.

He repeated, in a hesitating attitude and a timid voice:

'Have I not kept my promise I made you last night?'

He expected a word of thanks, a gesture at least, to prove the interest which she took in his action. She was silent.

Her scorn irritated Arsène Lupin, and at the same time he received a profound sense of all that separated him from Nellie, now that she knew the truth. He would have liked to exonerate himself, to seek excuses, to show his life in its bolder and greater aspects. But the words jarred upon him before they were uttered, and he felt the absurdity and the impertinence of any explanation. Then, overcome by a flood of memories, he murmured, sadly:

'How distant the past seems! Do you remember the long hours on the deck of the Provence? . . . Ah, stay . . . one day you had a rose in your hand, as you have today, a pale rose, like this one . . . I asked you for it . . . you seemed not to hear . . . However,

when you had gone below, I found the rose
. . . you had dropped it, no doubt . . . I have
kept it ever since . . . '

She still made no reply. She seemed very
far from him. He continued:

'For the sake of those dear hours, do not
think of what you know. Let the past be
joined to the present! Let me not be the man
whom you saw last night, but your fellow-
passenger on that voyage!'

She raised her eyes and looked at him as he
had requested. Then, without saying a word,
she pointed to a ring he was wearing on his
forefinger. Only the ring was visible; but the
setting, which was turned toward the palm of
his hand, consisted of a magnificent ruby.
Arsène Lupin blushed. The ring belonged to
Georges Devanne. He smiled bitterly, and
said:

'You are right. Nothing can be changed.
Arsène Lupin is now and always will be
Arsène Lupin. To you, he cannot be even so
much as a memory. Pardon me . . . I should
have known that any attention I may now
offer you is simply an insult. Forgive me.'

He stepped aside, hat in hand. Nelly passed
before him. He was inclined to detain her and
beseech her forgiveness. But his courage
failed, and he contented himself by following
her with his eyes, as he had done when she

descended the gangway to the pier at New York. She mounted the steps leading to the door, and disappeared within the house. He saw her no more.

A cloud obscured the sun. Arsène Lupin stood watching the imprints of her tiny feet in the sand. Suddenly, he gave a start. Upon the box which contained the bamboo, beside which Nelly had been standing, he saw the rose, the white rose which he had so coveted but dared not ask for. Forgotten, no doubt, also! But how — designedly or through distraction? He seized it eagerly. Some of its petals fell to the ground. He picked them up, one by one, like precious relics.

'Come!' he said to himself. 'I have nothing more to do here. I must think of my safety, before Sherlock Holmes arrives.'

The park was deserted, but some gendarmes were stationed at the park-gate. He entered a grove of pine trees, leaped over the wall, and, as a short cut to the railroad station, followed a path across the fields. After walking about ten minutes, he arrived at a spot where the road grew narrower and ran between two steep banks. In this ravine, he met a man travelling in the opposite direction. It was a man about fifty years of age, tall, smooth-shaven, and wearing clothes of a foreign cut. He carried a heavy cane, and a small satchel was strapped across his shoulder. When they met, the stranger spoke, with a slight English accent:

'Excuse me, monsieur, is this the way to the castle?'

'Yes, monsieur, straight ahead, and turn to the left when you come to the wall. They are expecting you.'

'Ah!'

'Yes, my friend Devanne told us last night that you were coming, and I am delighted to be the first to welcome you. Sherlock Holmes has no more ardent admirer than . . . myself.'

There was a touch of irony in his voice that he quickly regretted, for Sherlock Holmes scrutinized him from head to foot with such a keen, penetrating eye that Arsène Lupin experienced the sensation of being seized, imprisoned and registered by that look more thoroughly and precisely than he had ever been by a camera.

'My negative is taken now,' he thought, 'and it will be useless to use a disguise with that man. He would look right through it. But, I wonder, has he recognized me?'

They bowed to each other as if about to part. But, at that moment, they heard a sound of horses' feet, accompanied by a clinking of steel. It was the gendarmes. The two men were obliged to draw back against the embankment, amongst the bushes, to avoid the horses. The gendarmes passed by, but, as they followed each other at a considerable distance, they were several minutes in doing so. And Lupin was thinking:

'It all depends on that question: has he recognized me? If so, he will probably take advantage of the opportunity. It is a trying situation.'

When the last horseman had passed, Sherlock Holmes stepped forth and brushed the dust from his clothes. His bag caught on a branch and Lupin leaned forward to help loose him. Then, for a moment, he and Arsène Lupin gazed at each other; and, if a person could have seen them at that moment, it would have been an interesting sight, and memorable as the first meeting of two remarkable men, so strange, so powerfully equipped, both of superior quality, and destined by fate, through their peculiar attributes, to hurl themselves one at the other like two equal forces that nature opposes, one against the other, in the realms of space.

Then the Englishman said: 'Thank you, monsieur.'

'You are quite welcome,' replied Arsène Lupin.

They parted. Lupin went toward the

railway station, and Sherlock Holmes continued on his way to the castle.

The local officers had given up the investigation after several hours of fruitless efforts, and the people at the castle were awaiting the arrival of the English detective with a lively curiosity. At first sight, they were a little disappointed on account of his commonplace appearance, which differed so greatly from the pictures they had formed of him in their own minds. He did not in any way resemble the romantic hero, the mysterious and diabolical personage that the name of Sherlock Holmes had evoked in their imaginations. However, M. Devanne exclaimed, with great gusto:

'Ah! Monsieur, you are here! I am delighted to see you. It is a long-deferred pleasure. Really, I scarcely regret what has happened, since it affords me the opportunity to meet you. But, how did you come?'

'By the train.'

'But I sent my automobile to meet you at the station.'

'An official reception, eh? With music and fireworks! Oh, no! Not for me. That is not the way I do business,' grumbled the Englishman.

This speech disconcerted Devanne, who replied, with a forced smile:

'Fortunately, the business has been greatly simplified since I wrote to you.'

'In what way?'

'The robbery took place last night.'

'If you had not announced my intended visit, it is probable the robbery would not have been committed last night.'

'When, then?'

'Tomorrow, or some other day.'

'And in that case?'

'Lupin would have been trapped.'

'And my furniture?'

'Would not have been carried away.'

'Ah! But my goods are here. They were brought back at three o'clock.'

'By Lupin?'

'By two army-wagons.'

Sherlock Holmes put on his cap and adjusted his satchel. Devanne exclaimed anxiously:

'But, monsieur, what are you going to do?'

'I am going home.'

'Why?'

'Your goods have been returned; Arsène Lupin is far away — there is nothing for me to do.'

'Yes, there is. I need your assistance. What happened yesterday may happen again tomorrow, as we do not know how he entered, or how he escaped, or why, a few hours later, he returned the goods.'

'Ah! You don't know — '

The idea of a problem to be solved quickened the interest of Sherlock Holmes.

'Very well, let us make a search — at once — and alone, if possible.'

Devanne understood, and conducted the Englishman to the salon. In a dry, crisp voice, in sentences that seemed to have been prepared in advance, Holmes asked a number of questions about the events of the preceding evening, and enquired also concerning the guests and the members of the household. Then he examined the two volumes of the 'Chronique,' compared the plans of the subterranean passage, requested a repetition of the sentences discovered by Father Gélis, and then asked:

'Was yesterday the first time you have spoken of those two sentences to anyone?'

'Yes.'

'You have never communicated them to Horace Velmont?'

'No.'

'Well, order the automobile. I must leave in an hour.'

'In an hour?'

'Yes; within that time, Arsène Lupin solved the problem that you placed before him.'

'I . . . I placed before him — '

'Yes, Arsène Lupin or Horace Velmont — same thing.'

'I thought so. Ah! The scoundrel!'

'Now, let us see,' said Holmes, 'last night at ten o'clock, you furnished Lupin with the information that he lacked, and that he had been seeking for many weeks. During the night, he found time to solve the problem, collect his men, and rob the castle. I shall be quite as expeditious.'

He walked from end to end of the room, in deep thought, then sat down, crossed his long legs, and closed his eyes.

Devanne waited, quite embarrassed. Thought he:

'Is the man asleep? Or is he only meditating?'

However, he left the room to give some orders, and when he returned he found the detective on his knees scrutinizing the carpet at the foot of the stairs in the gallery.

'What is it?' he enquired.

'Look . . . there . . . spots from a candle.'

'You are right — and quite fresh.'

'And you will also find them at the top of the stairs, and around the cabinet that Arsène Lupin broke into, and from which he took the knick-knacks that he afterwards placed in this armchair.'

'What do you conclude from that?'

'Nothing. These facts would doubtless explain the cause for the restitution, but that is a side issue that I cannot wait to investigate. The main question is the secret passage. First, tell me, is there a chapel some two or three hundred metres from the castle?'

'Yes, a ruined chapel, containing the tomb of Duke Rollo.'

'Tell your chauffeur to wait for us near the chapel.'

'My chauffeur hasn't returned. If he had, they would have informed me. Do you think the secret passage runs to the chapel? What reason have — '

'I would ask you, monsieur,' interrupted the detective, 'to furnish me with a ladder and a lantern.'

'What! Do you require a ladder and a lantern?'

'Certainly, or I shouldn't have asked for them.'

Devanne, somewhat disconcerted by this crude logic, rang the bell. The two articles were brought. The succeeding orders were given with the sternness and precision of military commands.

'Place the ladder against the bookcase, to the left of the word Thibermesnil.'

Devanne placed the ladder as directed, and the Englishman continued:

'More to the left . . . to the right . . . there!
Now, climb up . . . All the letters are in relief,
aren't they?'

'Yes.'

'First, turn the letter 'I' one way or the
other.'

'Which one?' There are two of them.'

'The first one.'

Devanne took hold of the letter, and
exclaimed:

'Ah! Yes, it turns toward the right. Who told
you that?'

Sherlock Holmes did not reply to the
question, but continued his directions:

'Now, take the letter 'B'. Move it back and
forth as you would a bolt.'

Devanne did so, and, to his great surprise,
it produced a clicking sound.

'Quite right,' said Holmes. 'Now, we will go
to the other end of the word Thibermesnil,
try the letter 'I', and see if it will open like a
wicket.'

With a certain degree of solemnity,
Devanne seized the letter. It opened, but
Devanne fell from the ladder, for the entire
section of the bookcase, lying between the
first and last letters of the word, turned on a
pivot and disclosed the subterranean
passage.

Sherlock Holmes said, coolly:

'You are not hurt?'

'No, no,' said Devanne, as he rose to his feet, 'not hurt, only bewildered. I can't understand how . . . those letters turn . . . the secret passage opens . . . '

'Certainly. Doesn't that agree exactly with the formula given by Sully? Turn one eye on the bee that shakes, the other eye will lead to God.'

'But Louis XVI.?'

'Louis XVI. was a clever locksmith. I have read a book he wrote about combination locks. It was a good idea on the part of the owner of Thibermesnil to show to His Majesty a clever bit of mechanism. As an aid to his memory, the king wrote: 3–4–11, that is to say, the third, fourth, and eleventh letters of the word.'

'Exactly. I understand that. It explains how Lupin got out of the room, but it does not explain how he entered. And it is certain that he came from the outside.'

Sherlock Holmes lighted his lantern, and stepped into the passage.

'Look! All the mechanism is exposed here, like the works of a clock, and the reverse side of the letters can be reached. Lupin worked the combination from this side — that is all.'

'What proof is there of that?'

'Proof? Why, look at the puddle of oil.

Lupin foresaw even that the wheels would require oiling.'

'Did he know about the other entrance?'

'As well as I know it,' said Holmes. 'Follow me.'

'Into that dark passage?'

'Are you afraid?'

'No, but are you sure you can find the way out?'

'With my eyes closed.'

At first, they descended twelve steps, then twelve more, and, farther on, two other flights of twelve steps each. Then they walked through a long passageway, the brick walls of which showed the marks of successive restorations, and, in spots, were dripping with water. The earth, also, was very damp.

'We are passing under the pond,' said Devanne, somewhat nervously.

At last, they came to a stairway of twelve steps, followed by three others of twelve steps each, which they mounted with difficulty, and then found themselves in a small cavity cut into the rock. They could go no farther.

'The deuce!' muttered Holmes, 'nothing but bare walls. This is provoking.'

'Let us go back,' said Devanne. 'I have seen enough to satisfy me.'

But the Englishman raised his eyes and uttered a sigh of relief. There, he saw the same mechanism and the same word as before. He had merely to work the three letters. He did so, and a block of granite swung out of place. On the other side, this granite block formed the tombstone of Duke Rollo, and the word 'Thibermesnil' was engraved on it in relief. Now, they were in the little ruined chapel, and the detective said:

'The other eye leads to God; that means, to the chapel.'

'It is marvellous!' exclaimed Devanne, amazed at the clairvoyance and vivacity of the Englishman. 'Can it be possible that those few words were sufficient for you?'

'Bah!' declared Holmes. 'They weren't even necessary. In the chart in the book of the Bibliothéque Nationale, the drawing terminates at the left, as you know, in a circle, and at the right, as you do not know, in a cross. Now, that cross must refer to the chapel in which we now stand.'

Poor Devanne could not believe his ears. It was all so new, so novel to him. He exclaimed:

'It is incredible, miraculous, and yet of a childish simplicity! How is it that no one has ever solved the mystery?'

'Because no one has ever united the essential elements, that is to say, the two books and the two sentences. No one, but

Arsène Lupin and myself.'

'But, Father Gélis and I knew all about those things, and, likewise — '

Holmes smiled, and said:

'Monsieur Devanne, not everybody can solve riddles.'

'I have been trying for ten years to accomplish what you did in ten minutes.'

'Bah! I am used to it.'

They emerged from the chapel, and found an automobile.

'Ah! There's an auto waiting for us.'

'Yes, it is mine,' said Devanne.

'Yours? You said your chauffeur hadn't returned.'

They approached the machine, and M. Devanne questioned the chauffeur:

'Edouard, who gave you orders to come here?'

'Why, it was Monsieur Velmont.'

'M. Velmont? Did you meet him?'

'Near the railway station, and he told me to come to the chapel.'

'To come to the chapel! What for?'

'To wait for you, monsieur, and your friend.'

Devanne and Holmes exchanged looks, and M. Devanne said:

'He knew the mystery would be a simple one for you. It is a delicate compliment.'

A smile of satisfaction lighted up the detective's serious features for a moment. The compliment pleased him. He shook his head, as he said:

'A clever man! I knew that when I saw him.'

'Have you seen him?'

'I met him a short time ago — on my way from the station.'

'And you knew it was Horace Velmont — I mean, Arsène Lupin?'

'No, but I supposed it was — from a certain ironical speech he made.'

'And you allowed him to escape?'

'Of course I did. And yet I had everything on my side, such as five gendarmes who passed us.'

'Sacrebleu!' cried Devanne. 'You should have taken advantage of the opportunity.'

'Really, monsieur,' said the Englishman, haughtily, 'when I encounter an adversary like Arsène Lupin, I do not take advantage of chance opportunities, I create them.'

But time pressed, and since Lupin had been so kind as to send the automobile, they resolved to profit by it. They seated themselves in the comfortable limousine; Edouard took his place at the wheel, and away they went toward the railway station. Suddenly, Devanne's eyes fell upon a small package in one of the pockets of the carriage.

'Ah! What is that? A package! Whose is it? Why, it is for you.'

'For me?'

'Yes, it is addressed: 'Sherlock Holmes, from Arsène Lupin.''

'The Englishman took the package, opened it, and found that it contained a watch.

'Ah!' he exclaimed, with an angry gesture.

'A watch,' said Devanne. 'How did it come there?'

The detective did not reply.

'Oh! It is your watch! Arsène Lupin returns your watch! But, in order to return it, he must have taken it. Ah! I see! He took your watch! That is a good one! Sherlock Holmes' watch stolen by Arsène Lupin! Mon Dieu! That is funny! Really . . . you must excuse me . . . I can't help it.'

He roared with laughter, unable to control himself. After which, he said, in a tone of earnest conviction: 'A clever man, indeed!'

The Englishman never moved a muscle. On the way to Dieppe, he never spoke a word, but fixed his gaze on the flying landscape. His silence was terrible, unfathomable, more violent than the wildest rage. At the railway station, he spoke calmly, but in a voice that impressed one with the vast energy and will power of that famous man. He said:

'Yes, he is a clever man, but some day I shall have the pleasure of placing on his shoulder the hand I now offer to you, Monsieur Devanne. And I believe that Arsène Lupin and Sherlock Holmes will meet again some day. Yes, the world is too small — we will meet — we must meet — and then — '